Summer's Lease

Sara Clark

To Rusty —

My kinda god!,

Love
Sara
—x—

To Bill and Peggy Armitage

With all my love

3

Chapter One

Looking out into the black emptiness beyond the glass, it's hard to believe there's a garden out there. Hard to believe there's anything but that flat black square of sky, the scent of damp on the windowsill, my own two eyes peering out. If I could snap my fingers and make it morning now, I'd see it all there, and feel something perhaps. Long grass rippling in the summer breeze, the scent of rain still wet on the hedgerows, little silvery drops of it exploding out as the crows land on their branches. But it's night now, and I've finally made my mind up to write about the house, get the whole ordeal out of the way. I suppose I'll have to more or less guess how big the garden is - Dad always said half an acre at the front and four at the back, that's not counting the meadow, and then there's the private woodland beside the driveway, can't forget that.

Fifty or so tall pine trees surround the bluebell glade.

There, I've started writing it. A hammock hung there once, and could again I guess, if I had the patience to cut a path through the hogweed and into the centre of it. As it stands, that task will be left to someone else. Someone who's being paid to do it, I don't have the time.

Dad used to love doing stuff like that, hands-on, get it done, job's a good-un, and I've got to say I respected him for it, tending to our private forest with its little eco-system of crows, nettles, bones and branches, not to mention those pungently delicate little stars of wild garlic flowers which I used to love to eat. Oh, there are all kinds of flowers in that forest - marshmallow, rhododendron, I have so many memories of those vivid blooms - soft, wet and rotten at the edges. There are things to hide behind

5

too, things hidden within things, tiny piles of rodent skulls littered about the foxholes, and round the back, the willow tree. But let's stick to the front lawn for now.

The front garden has a sunny aspect and is kept separate from the main road by a deep ditch through which a miniature brook runs in the wetter months. The flower beds that skirt the garden yield thickets of lavender, chives, mint, and thyme, and flowering cherry trees thick with fruit can be enjoyed in springtime.

Ah, who knows how much of this is true anymore, underneath all those nettles. There are some gardening gloves in the shed and it might be the right weather for pulling them all up in the morning but god knows I'm not going to do it. The rain outside's enchanting. Listen to it, gurgling through the gutters like that. I ought to have written this sooner, in the daytime, so I could see it all for myself instead of relying on my memory, because I'm too tired and drunk to recollect it all correctly at this time of night.

A large cherry tree shelters an array of flowers in the centre of the garden, which, whilst facing the main road, has a pleasant and sunny aspect hearkening back to the times of tennis, backgammon and afternoon tea. To the left of this magnificent English garden lies a secluded private forest, alive with all the flora and fauna of the English woodlands.

English - that's a good word to use twice, such *nostalgia* attached to it. Cream teas, picnic baskets, white sheets, lavender, china cups, and ping-pong on the lawn. No, not ping-pong. Table tennis. Dad was a champion if the stories are to be believed, although I never saw him play against an actual *adult*. God, listen to the rain, it's howling out there too, I'll wake up and the whole property will have washed away, there'll be nothing left to sell. I'm

6

alone out here in the middle of nowhere. It's too dark outside to be doing this, so why am I in the mood?

In between the wood and the garden lies a fenced gravel path leading to a driveway in which three vehicles can be parked comfortably. Resplendent hedgerows grow at either side of the fence, lending a magical quality to the approach, which, with its wealth of daffodils and red berries beckons one in as though through an enchanted tunnel of undergrowth.

To think I never wrote before tonight, eh Dad? I ought to crank out some tunes on that old boom box of yours - Tina Turner, M People, all your favourite girls standing in the wings just waiting to belt out a tune, keep me company. But there it is again. That voice, that insufferable dragging of heels inside me. I simply *can't be bothered.*

Secreted at the very edge of the forest is a sizeable pond, freshly stocked with koi carp and often visited by a local heron. Lending the pond an impressionistic quality are a surplus of colourful water-lilies, reeds and dragonflies.

Damn fine pond my father dug. Many's the time I've stood by it, peering into its opalescent green depths and thinking things over. There's a greengage tree just beside it, and they fall in, these unusual fruits with their purple tops, bobbing about in there. Talk about a Garden of Eden, they'll snap this place up once I list it properly. Who'd have thought I had a gift for description? The words are pouring out of me, ripe with promise.

A gentle white mist of daisies can be found hovering across the back lawn, and in winter, the silver frost sparkles across it like a thick sheet of silver. At the very front of the garden, a red Japanese maple watches over a number of graves, which are to be preserved in their

7

original state by the buyer. These are family graves and as such the sole condition of sale is that the new owner under no circumstances attempts to relocate their inhabitants, each of whom expressed an ardent wish to remain interred in the hallowed grounds of the house which they so loved.

I wonder if there's a better way of putting the word 'graves' in there? It's a sombre word, but there's something lovely about it too. It's imposing - it means something. *The grey stone graves of long dead family members.* No, you see, that last bit ruins it. They were people, after all, not disembodied limbs. Dad's told me all about them – how Granny Maude paced around the living room on the day of our first garden burial in that crumpled black velvet coat she left to my mother, scaring the life out of my uncle Jack.

He was a miserable young man, terrified of everything, and for one reason or another couldn't work up the nerve to go outside for his father's funeral, which was ironic, as the only reason they were burying him in the garden in the first place was so Jack could attend. Agoraphobia, but Maude had persuaded him he'd make it from one end of the garden to the other. Persuaded herself, more like.

When I imagine that day, I can see the whole scene in my head very clearly. I've got a good ear for voices, speech patterns, accents, anything like that. When I say a good ear I mean a genuine talent, Dad always said I could have been an actor. So when I tell you my granny Maude said "I have moved heaven and earth to have this happen Jack Warren!" seventy years ago in the very same room I'm standing in now, you have very good reason to believe she said just that. Jack was my *dad's* brother, by the way, and he lived in the room just behind me for the best part of his life. A shut-in, like a few others I could mention.

"I have moved heaven and earth, and if you can't make the effort to come pay your last respects to your father at this very difficult time, I'm afraid to say I will have lost my patience with you completely!"

I imagine she yelled this while straightening up a gilt-edged plate of hors d'oeuvres. Big on baking, Maude was, and she had a particular flair for buffets which meant that most of the family funerals I attended up until 1980 were very happy affairs, with flowers, and ice buckets, and mile-long lines of sandwiches in various flavours. Good god how I loved those sandwiches! None of your vegan nonsense.

"What's the big deal about, he's just in the garden?" Jack frowned, picking a piece of pink meat from the centre of a vol-au-vent and holding it up to the window for inspection. "Are these *prawns*?"

"Do you think I wanted to bury him in the garden of our cottage? No. I wanted him in a sodding cemetery, I arranged all of this because you were afraid to be left alone in the house while we went to the funeral, end of story! And yes, they are prawns, is that a problem?" It was the eyes he wouldn't have liked, by the way, and those little pink whiskers, god knows what they're called. The way they curl, the scales, the frail translucent shells that stuck to his fingers. The guy was a big insect lover.

Jack grimaced and took an ornately folded napkin from the stack, wrapping a pastry in it. "You could have at least made the ham ones."

"Oh could I? Thanks for the tip! Maybe if you could be bothered to come outside, I might consider making more of an effort with the catering at the next funeral we might happen to have here!" Maude folded a napkin into an ornamental swan as she spoke.

"I'm *not* going outside," Jack winced through gritted teeth. I think that my brother George actually picked up this habit from Uncle Jack personally, after all, the fellow practically raised him, living at home with us all his life and keeping him company in the living room until late most nights. George dropped out of school when he was only eight, you see, and he often used to stay up late watching terrible TV shows with Uncle Jack long after everyone else was in bed.

"Yes, you *are* going outside!" Maude cried. "All of this is on your account Jack, and if you can't haul your narrow behind into some black clothes and stagger a few feet out of the front door for your own father's funeral, I swear I will disown you. Look at the effort your brother has gone to! He's put you to shame, standing guard over Dad with poise and dignity, and there you are, practically wandering around in your underwear with him lying dead in the garden!" Now the women in my family are prone to extreme exaggeration and it's by no means taking liberties when I say Maude would accuse him of walking around nude if she thought it would get a reaction, but she was too prudish for that - at least, if she was anything like my mother, to whom socks, pants, bras, G-strings and thongs alike were all simply 'underthings'.

"Would you please just stop whining?" Jack squealed, stamping past her.

"Fine," Maude said, pressing her feet into her new black patent heels and admiring them for a moment. Now this might be a liberty on my part but I do remember Dad saying how much *someone* liked their shoes, whether it was my mother in her younger days or Maude at the height of her sexual powers as a woman, I am honestly not sure. But isn't it a pretty image? The image of Maude sinking into the mud in those shiny patent heels, the image of Maude in heels bought with the dirty proceeds of her husband's life insurance money. The more I think of this image, the more fitting it is, the more appropriate to the rich symbolism of the anecdote, the gradual sinking into the ground wherein her husband is interred, the slow, faltering steps of the widow, a woman whose true feelings about her dead husband were never truly exhumed from that dark tomb of a heart of hers. Before she left, she looked over her shoulder.

"Jack, I won't forget this, do you understand me? I'm done with you. You're on your own from now on, do you hear?"

"Whatever, just stop yelling would you woman?" the muffled voice replied. Now you see, if this were a scene between my mother and George (and I can confidently assure you many such scenes have taken place within these walls) his voice would have been muffled because he was locked in his room playing his computer games, but Uncle Jack didn't have the good luck to be born in such an age. Whatever he got up to in there you can bet it wasn't fun. Blackjack or 'razzle mags', maybe he liked to paint, but god, it's impossible to imagine how he coped without an electrical gadget of any description. Even 'Pong', didn't come out until twenty years afterwards!

Meanwhile, by the graveside, Bill, his long hair shorn off to commemorate the occasion, stared up at the yellow-edged streaks of cloud that hovered above the ploughed brown earth. What a dreadful place to be buried it must have seemed back then, before it became the family

11

norm, I mean – laid cold and alone in a flowerless garden with only a few ravens as companions. It's much improved now, with all the gnomes, photographs and little plastic windmills Mother put there.

Maude tramped through the mud until she reached the very edge of the garden by the main road. Do you see in your mind's eye now, the very same garden I described at the beginning of this story? I imagine that there was something almost festive about the bare wintry scene before them on that day, and that the scrunched up crisp packets that random passers-by had wedged between the dark boughs of bramble were glimmering like red, green and blue baubles. It is details like these that bring the whole thing home in technicolour.

After a few moments' silence, Maude began to speak.

"Frank lived and died doing exactly what he wanted to do and it was very forward-thinking of him to take out such a comprehensive life insurance policy. I'm sorry if that sounds rather callous but it is an undeniable fact that we're now financially secure and I think that Frank did that for us on purpose. In return we will guard his fortress and keep his grave a sacred place." She struggled to reposition her weight as her heels sank into the mud. "Now, Frank was a frugal man who liked the simple things in life, and with that in mind I decided to have him buried in this very simple cardboard coffin." I will be completely honest here and let you know that at this stage of the story, Maude has become my mother, Margaret. "I am sure he would have found it most appropriate."

Margaret turned stiffly toward Bill, who was staring at the cardboard box. "I believe you had a few words to say Bill?" she muttered. Bill stepped forward.

Now this is where it gets complicated, as suddenly in my mind's eye, it is not Frank, but *my father himself* who is being buried by Margaret, and so, in keeping with the story, the young version of Bill has morphed into none other than yours truly – Alex Warren – son to Bill and Margaret Warren, brother to George.

"Just one word actually, Mother," I said, "and that word is *why?* Why the hell is Bill Warren, a relatively harmless individual who had the rest of his life ahead of him being buried in his front garden today? Was it his love of the Suffolk countryside? His contemplative disposition? No, I'm afraid the answer is a little less romantic. He's being buried in the garden because George was too afraid of leaving the house to go to the local cemetery for the funeral. My mother, in her naivety, thought it would be a great idea to hold the ceremony here so both his children could attend. Burying him in the garden he adored, so he could be near his beloved family. There's only one problem with that bright idea. We all hated him."

"Alex!" Mum began, no doubt realising I was right.

"Which brings me on to my next point. The reason he died. Now, the fact is, my father had nothing left to live for. His wife couldn't stand the sight of him and his kids were ungrateful brats who resented him for the part he played in their existence. He had zero self-esteem and didn't respect himself in the slightest. Neither did anyone else."

A car drove past, tooting its horn in a jovial rhythm, and as the gravediggers turned to glare at it I crouched on the floor, pressing my palm into the damp soil and watching the green grass gleam through the spaces between my fingers. A bird-scarer sounded out a shot in the distance, sending a clumsy handful of crows into the air and knocking the speech I'd rehearsed clean out of my head.

"We spent a lot of time together in this garden – did things I never thought of until now – climbing trees, picking apples, cutting the grass with that bloody great scythe over there, building igloos when it snowed... did those things really happen, here, on this green lawn? It's hard to believe that they did. You know, I actually feel closer to Dad now that he's a corpse in a cardboard box than I ever did when he was alive, in a meadow, kicking a ball toward me. I won't pretend I'm going to miss him much, *none of us will*, but I *am* incredibly sad about how it all ended."

I looked at my mother for perhaps the first time that afternoon. She had loosened her scarf and was twisting it around her fingers, gazing up at the cottage window from which George's curious face now gleamed, peering through the net curtains. I ran my fingers through my freshly-cut fringe, then pointed at the sand-coloured carton that held my father's body.

"Take a look at that monstrosity," I said. "He was denied his dignity right down to the last detail. *Goldfish* around England have better lives, *and get better funerals* than his – the man is being buried in a *cardboard box* for Christ's sake. I know for a fact that if this was a funeral for a dead fish instead of a human being, George would be the one reading out the eulogy right now - but he's too damaged to care about anything larger than a first-class postage stamp. We're all too damaged to deal with any of this. We're beyond hope, the lot of us. Why not bury Dad as if he were a pet, eh? It's a fitting tribute. He lived without purpose, he died for no reason, and nothing whatsoever has been learned from the fact that he ever existed. Except, obviously, never to get married or have kids. Now if you'll excuse me, I'm going to my room."

I suppose the question you must have about my little story is which is the truer of the two halves, the beginning or the end? Well, as the saying goes, that's for me to know and you to find out. It's really pouring it down outside now, in a way that makes me wish it would rain forever, the silent, unending whisper of the water soothing the wounds of the world with the gentle bubble and rasp of its tongue. It makes me want to sleep and to wake up young again, a baby wrapped up in blankets, ready to start it all over from the beginning, every goddamn awkward second of it.

Funny thing empathy – I mean, do you have to actually know living, breathing people to fully experience it or is it something you can imagine having? To me, having empathy is kind of like stepping inside a virtual reality machine and living life as someone else, except with the real stuff you have to use the power of your mind. It's really black outside, no point trying to write about the garden tonight. I'll make a start on the kitchen instead, it's much friendlier in there.

Situated at the Eastern-most edge of the house, with fine views of the pond to the east and the back meadow to the north is the kitchen, which was added by…

Now, who was the owner back in the mid-18th century? Dad would know. Mum too, for that matter, it was only me who never took an interest in the place. Ha!

With its quarry stone floor tiles and exposed wooden beams, this small but efficient kitchen is the perfect place to cook, relax, or simply recover from a hard day's toil in the company of loved ones and friends.

I'm so glad I got rid of that massive antique table. It used to really dominate the room and I was sick of walking into the edge of it. The chair by the fridge will suit me fine, besides, I usually eat standing up. Dad loved that table though - I remember he used to sprawl across it as soon as he got home with some favoured object still clasped in his hand - his keys, his reading glasses, or a bottle of ibuprofen. Then mum would bring him some steaming hot Earl Grey tea, wedging the cup into a tiny space she'd made among the stacks of tins, bottles, envelopes and vitamin supplements. Ah Mother! Forever fetching and carrying things that nobody really wanted! So many nights of our lives ended in an identical manner that it ought to be hard to remember this one in particular – I mean, the one that marked the end of my old life, but it's stuck in my mind despite everything I've done to exorcise it from my memory, like it's still happening, in this same place, so many years later.

The kitchen units are painted in an attractive cream colour and made of solid pine.

No, there's no use lying about the units, they're nearly as disgusting as the cooker. I never use any of them, that's the truth. There's probably grease on the hob still sitting there from that huge pan of sweet potato fritters Mum fried up twenty years ago. Now as far as food's concerned, I take after my dad, I mean - he would have been happy with a napkin and a burger for his supper but Mum always insisted on playing mother hen, rustling up some elaborate Delia-inspired feast of local, organic produce 'just because.'

16

Now I suppose that would have worked just fine for Dad if she'd been able to do it with a smile upon occasion, but she never served him food without making some passive aggressive remark about how little he did for her in return. Every night he'd come home, take his seat at the table with a bottle and gaze sheepishly up at her busy figure from the rim of his wine glass. I mean, he'd been at the office all day, and I really think she was oblivious to the fact that *he* worked hard for every penny *she* spent. Playing house is nice, *Mother*, but it doesn't pay for the repairs - the endless succession of builders, plumbers and glaziers necessary to make a house into a home. Dad understood that.

Dad used to have a real love-hate relationship with this kitchen. I mean, he spent hours drunkenly examining it through half-closed eyes, visibly disturbed by some small flaw or another. It was basically a motel to visiting insects of all kinds. I'm talking about the endless varieties of spiders, lice and centipedes that used to crawl out of holes and creep across the carpets on dark, wet nights like this one. Of course back then there was the stench too – something a little like the damp in the air tonight, but with a rotten edge to it, and the ground beneath the loose tiles was always riddled with black mould.

The two large kitchen windows allow for a plentiful amount of light to enter the room at all times of day and offer unparalleled views of the surrounding English countryside.

At night, they are black eyes, peering inward. Dad wasn't a particularly sensitive man, but I get the feeling it wasn't just the look of the kitchen that disturbed him - it wasn't just the cold of it, the decrepitude, the slanting ceilings, loose steps, holes in walls, or piles of objet d'art stacked everywhere. It was the fact that the kitchen was the place

17

where he *looked* at himself - his own personal portrait of Dorian Gray. The house was nothing less than a measure of his success as a man - a reflection of his physical decrepitude. The collapsed roof was his buckled spine, the un-flushable toilet was his bowels, and the windows were his yellow corneas.

On this particular night, Mum was making gluten-free Quorn lasagna while Dad 'looked at himself' in the way I've just described. Dad was a very reflective person and there's no doubt he believed that if he restored the house to its former glory singlehandedly, his family would forever remember him as a man who got things done. He never actually *told* us he loved us – no, that would have been too easy. He planned to *show* us, with the home improvements he was crippling himself to make, the ways that we could better love ourselves. Living in a good home, with hope and self-respect, he genuinely believed we would lose that ghastly look of sacrifice which was our trademark. One day he would die, but the house would stand proud – a beacon to guide his sons to safety through the dark times of their lives.

Anyway, as my father sat at the table, the clatter of a pan snapped him out of his contemplative state, and soon afterwards he lifted his wine bottle to let my mother wipe the table. While she cleaned and tutted, Dad looked up at the ceiling, clearly seeing something else, something cleaner. Back then the room was a dingy rectangle of buckled walls, broken windows and low, bent beams of oak, and thanks to my mum's hoarding instinct, it had a tacky feel to it that was in direct opposition to my father's love for clean lines and bare-bones architecture. Decorative bits of chintz seemed to blossom from the walls themselves – framed dried flowers and needle-point pictures randomly nailed into place, and I imagine the only way Dad coped with this prolific abundance of jumble was to somehow see through it to the sleek, restored wall he envisioned beneath it.

I followed his gaze to the pantry to discover George standing there.

"Making dinner?" Dad asked. George had adopted the same hunched posture and blank facial expression as Mother over the years, something I was careful to avoid, despite the decades I'd spent living with her. He was wearing his bobbled grey fleece that night, paired with ill-fitting jeans which betrayed no trace of leg or knee beneath their threadbare folds. I had a similar outfit myself, but wore it less often, as Dad hated to see us dressed so scruffily and often remarked upon how unhappy it made him. "I don't mean to sound rude, George, but do you ever change your clothes?" he asked. "They have new ones at the shops, you know. I could get you some if you like?"

"You think money solves everything, don't you?" George snapped, opening a packet of gluten-free cornflakes and examining one in disgust. These tiny little scraps of sugared corn were an absolute last measure for the sweet-toothed seeker of treats in our house, and eating just one of them would have been like inflating the last lifeboat on a sinking yacht. "Have you seen that muesli bar, Dad? I think there's one spare. I was saving it for later but I think I'll have it for me supper." My brother had a peculiarity of pronouncing certain words in a working-class accent, learned from TV as a child.

"I didn't eat it, that's for sure," Dad said.

"If that's true, it's the only thing you didn't eat. You had all the gluten-free hot cross buns before tea today, then came back for the chocolate rice cakes. You ate three. I saw you eating them in the living room."

The pantry was usually crammed from top to bottom with fruit flakes, yoghurt-coated soy beans, wasabi peas, organic liquorice and the like, but this particular incident happened during the same month my mother set her mind on emptying Grandad's old stuff from the house she'd inherited from him, so tensions in the household were high as she'd neglected her shopping duties. Once she set her mind on a project like that it was a case of 'to hell with the lot of you' where shopping was concerned, and instead of bringing home things we could eat without any fuss, she insisted on controlling us further by cooking a set meal when she returned, and nothing more. You understand, then, that the last muesli bar in the house at this stage of the game was no mere biscuit to George.

"Well, I didn't eat your muesli bar, you can be sure of that."

It was easy to lie to George, who was incapable of thinking about another person's point of view for long enough to consider whether or not they were telling the truth.

"Mind your backs, please, everyone!" Mum pulled the oven door open and it landed on its hinges with a great thud.

"Easy, easy, you'll have the door off its hinges at that rate, woman!"

20

"And you would know all about that Bill, having just smashed the conservatory window dragging that ruddy great sledgehammer in there."

This is a perfect example of the way Mother used to talk – in one single sentence chastising, condemning and deriding not only the man, but his actions, his desires, his very essence, simply because he'd been audacious enough to start up a conversation with her - the woman he'd tirelessly dedicated his life to in the vain hope that she might one day respect him.

Dad gulped down his wine. "Lovely bit of kit, that sledgehammer. Served its last master well."

"Yes, I'm sure it did, I'm sure it will be very pleased indeed to be left rusting away in a glass outhouse until we're all dead and buried," she sneered, trowelling a piece of lasagna onto a plate of fresh vegetables.

Now you can say what you like about my mother, but she was an excellent cook – and so English with it, I mean Royal Doulton, Paddington Bear, taking tea on the lawn - English in a way that you rarely see these days, and her lasagna, whilst Italian in name, was a perfect example of that quintessential Englishness one only discovers in kitchens such as the one she used to keep.

"Incidentally Margaret, iron doesn't rust, it oxidises, and the whole point of putting it in the conservatory…"

"The conservatory, the conservatory…" George whined, "I'm sick of hearing about the conservatory. What's the point of filling a stupid conservatory full of *stupid* things you're never going to use? Hang on, what's that wrapper in your pocket? Did you eat my last muesli bar?"

"I'll go get you some more, OK?"

"That's not the POINT!" George yelled, "Why doesn't anybody UNDERSTAND? I trusted you and you lied to me! How am I supposed to live here with a bunch of thieves and LIARS ruining my plans all the time? I mean, what are you even doing here, Dad?"

"I beg your pardon?"

"You heard me," George said, "The only reason you ever come back is to get your stuff washed, dump your rubbish all over our house and act like the big hero for the evening. Well, I'm sick of it!" And with that he marched out of the kitchen.

Adjacent to the kitchen is a drawing room with several original features, including open stud walls, traditional wall coverings and a wood-burning fire.

This room used to serve as a halfway house between the kitchen and the living room, a place for taking off shoes, dumping buckets of coal and shopping bags. There was a sofa and a rug beside the grand piano, and sometimes we'd set up a chess board on a footstool, Dad and I, and I'd sit cross-legged on the floor and let him win as he drank his wine by the fire.

I was about to go after George and tell him to apologise when Dad grabbed my sleeve.

"Leave him, leave him. It gives us a bit of time together," he said, "Come into the drawing room with me… come on, I'll show you something!"

He was drunk, at this stage, and I knew what was coming next.

"It's going to be amazing in here when I'm finished renovating it - see that wood beam? Would you believe me if I told you it was one solid piece of oak? Antique. Do you have any *idea* how expensive that would be to replace now?"

I didn't. I still don't. I remember his voice so well, it's like he's standing right behind me. I'm breathing deeply now, my eyes adjusting to the glare of the glass, and the black sky beyond the glass is beginning to bloom into deepest blue through the branches of the large pine. Oh Dad. Vines of ivy have begun to grow through the cracks in the windowsill – he'd have hated that. I swear I can still hear him, somewhere in the back of my mind.

"Except I'm not going to replace it. I'm going to pull it out and have it reworked into the wall of the house - over here. The architect said it couldn't be done, but… I don't want to patronise you if I can help it - how much do you know about joists, Alex? Nothing? Ah! Well, you've a quick mind, I'm sure you'll understand this…"

Dad had learnt this trick from his own father - throwing in a brief compliment at you in order to justify why he was about to spend an hour explaining something he knew *full well* you weren't interested in.

"See, the *architect* doesn't think this is going to work, but I came up with an invention that will let me take that whole piece out and make it into a rather nifty little joist." I sighed as he continued on, gazing at the antique grandfather clock by the door in order to retain some small amount of control over my actions. I ought to have known all about this clock, of course, as I'd been lectured on its origins and mechanisms the day before, but I'd been too busy staring at the ceiling at the time. "That's *engineering* for you," Dad said, "You never did study engineering - can't be helped – but I can teach you all about it if you want to know. You don't, of course. I know that."

I gazed at my father's face as he spoke – at the vast red web of veins that crept across his bulbous nose, and the broken blood vessels in his eyes. Tears were glistening on the mottled folds of leathery skin beneath his lids. A fresh flood of pity saturated my being.

"Yes, that sounds interesting, actually." I felt a twitch in my jaw as I said this – it felt like something elastic was snapping inside me.

"Oh, but it is. Fascinating stuff!" Dad wiped a tear from his eye with the corner of his handkerchief. "Tried explaining it to the other two but they were never interested." He sniffed, and turned his wounded face toward his me. "Course, I suppose you're not bothered either".

He was right, I wasn't.

"No, no, I like to learn new things," I said, ever the English gentleman. "So how would you get the joist out? I wouldn't know where to start!" I was now floating in a bubble of boredom inside of which all sense of moving forward had stopped, but at least I had someone to talk to. I wonder - if I turned around now and saw him standing there by the clock, looking exactly how he used to, what would I do differently? Could I bring myself to listen to the same damn speech one last time just to keep him happy?

"Ok, I have to pick up Dad's stamp collection, so when you've quite finished your little chat, please go get your lasagna before it goes cold," Mum interrupted, "If you'd like dessert, there's some apple pie in the oven and the custard's simmering on the hob." She gave a shy little smile and patted the oven as though it were a cherished pet. "I'll be back at about half past eleven, DON'T let George know I've gone out, if he asks where I am just say…"

"We know, we know…" Dad blurted out. "You've gone to bed – nudge, nudge… *wink, wink*!" He tapped the side of his nose.

"Bill, if you feel you must interrupt, can you at least do so quietly? George is just in the other room and if he hears I'm bringing more of Dad's old junk back into the house, he'll have a fit!"

"Fine… Bye then," Dad said as she crept out of the back door. He poked at the kitchen table for a while after she had gone, rearranging the mounds of catalogues, books and leaflets into one big messy pile and putting his plate down beside them. Then he sat down with a dejected look on his face, poking his fork into the steaming centre of the lasagna.

"It's so kind of her to make dinner for us," I said, trying to keep the peace between them.

"Yes," Dad mumbled through a mouthful of hot Quorn mince, "If only she could stop being *kind* and start being practical, this family might stand a chance of making it through the cold winter months."

He took a long swig of wine and filled his glass again.

"I leave you lot on your own for a single day and everything goes to pot. You'd all freeze to death if it wasn't for my trusty wood burner and amazing propensity for chopping firewood! Do you know, my father taught me how to chop firewood before I could even speak properly? Just another basic skill no bugger here grasps the importance of. Anyway, now your mother's out of the picture it's time to break this little beauty open."

He took a wine bottle from the counter and plonked it on the table.

"It's a Burgundy - costs me £18 a bottle. You should get a load of the guy who owns the deli I buy this from. His ears prick up when he sees me coming in. He can smell the money on me. He knows I always buy good stuff you see," Dad continued, "Of course, not all good wine is expensive. You can't buy class."

"Indeed, you cannot," I said.

"Unless, of course..." he said, reaching down beside him and pulling out a carrier bag, "You've just bought yourself one of these beauties. Take a look at this!" He pulled a bundle from the bag and shook it out. It was an orange coat. "Now *this*, my fine feathered friend, is fully waterproof Berghaus jacket. £170. They don't get better than this."

"Is this... for me?" I asked, amazed. Nobody ever bought me anything.

"Ha! You should be so lucky. Why would you need a waterproof jacket when you never go out? No, no, this little beauty's all mine. There's a storm tomorrow and I don't mean to get caught out in it on my way to work." He shoved the coat back into the bag and stood up. "*Is it for you?* Honestly!" He seemed to find the thought that I might wear a coat incredibly amusing. "I'll get you a glass. Lead crystal - see how well this is cut? That's how glasses USED to be made. Of course this is a sherry glass, I don't know why I took it out of the cupboard." He cupped the glass in his palm until his pink skin shone through it, blooming out beneath its facets. "Your mum used to love sherry.... almost as much as I loved her, in fact..."

He's losing it... I thought, stacking up the used plates and plunging them into the sink. The bubbles clung to my skin in irritating little circles and I was about to rinse them away when George pushed past me and began to scrub away at his plate with the plastic washing-up brush.

"Now this is what I don't understand," Dad began in a high, monotone drawl, "If you're making a decision to do something, why not do it properly?"

"What are you harping on about now?" George asked.

"The plate! I can understand leaving it out for someone else to wash, I can understand filling up the bowl with hot soapy water and doing the whole lot of them yourself - what I don't get is why you would use half measures - running a single bloody plate under the cold tap without soap, and expecting that brush to kill all the germs. It's not a magic wand you know."

"I was going to use soap."

27

"Yes, but if the water's not hot enough to burn your hand, it's not hot enough to kill germs. Basic physics."

Dad raised his glass in the air, toasting his own insight with gusto.

"Don't you mean biology?"

"Not important, you're missing my point. The fact is that you're… you're doing it wrong… that's all, just a bit of polite paternal advice, take it or leave it." He emptied the contents in a long swig.

"That's the only paternal advice you *ever* give me – that I'm doing it wrong." George tossed the washing up brush into the bowl. "Call yourself a father?" There was no trace of emotion in his voice.

"Don't leave the brush in the water like that, put it at the side of the sink so it can dry, for god's sake!"

"Leave me alone!" George cried. "I can't do anything in this house without someone noticing. I'm so miserable I feel like waking in front of a truck right now! In fact, I just might. Can someone give me one good reason why I shouldn't just go outside, right now and throw myself under a truck?"

"I've got one," I said.

"Go on then, what is it?" George challenged, "Why shouldn't I just go out and step in front of a truck? You tell me one good reason and maybe I won't do it!"

"You're agoraphobic," I grinned, taking a long swig from the bottle. Dad burst out laughing at this, and rightly so - it was one of the funniest wisecracks I ever made, and to be honest, the main reason I've taken the time to write this entire anecdote. I'm a huge Seinfeld fan, and always harboured a secret wish that we could be more like Elaine, George, Jerry and Kramer as a family. Jerry and Elaine used to date, but had grown into a platonic relationship, much like Mother and Father, and my brother shared both his name and defining traits with the neurotic control freak George Costanza. That made me Kramer – a misunderstood genius living off inherited money. I never did quite figure out how to make it work, but in moments such as the one I've just described, I believe we came close at times.

Chapter Two

The dark sky behind the storm clouds is shining blue now, just the slightest gleam of indigo beyond the black, and the stars will start to fade soon. If I opened the door and stepped outside into the rain, I wonder if I'd feel that same rush of adrenaline I used to get twenty years ago, my bare feet soaking up the roughness of the cold stone steps, as if standing on a diving board beneath which the whole world lay in wait.

After my dad's back pain meant he could no longer drive, a taxi would pull up into the driveway outside the house five days a week to take him to work. For years, in the early hours of morning I used to listen to him get ready from my bedroom, comforted by the bubble of the kettle, the dull metallic clank as he washed his coffee cup in the sink. The house was different back then – it felt like a tiny illuminated island floating in the safety of space, yellow tungsten lights piercing the galactic black expanse of the moonlit farmland, and it was in such moments of extreme contrast that I felt the joy of being alive most intensely. Somehow my life felt worth more to me on those cold, miserable early mornings than in the height of summer, when the cyan skies and dancing trees seem to insist that anything was possible. I have despised summer all my life – every summer but one, in fact. A summer where it rained so long and hard that, for a moment, everything was washed clean, the wet emerald gleam of leaves suddenly unsullied by insects.

I was always very wary of going out no matter which season it was – when people came too close to me, I got this overwhelming sense of dizziness, and a panic started up in my chest, like there was a bird trapped in there, beating its wings against my ribs to get out. When I was

30

younger Dad would sometimes sneak me out of the house and take me to town, and on those rare days I felt I was learning a lot from him. He had a way with people, speaking to strangers as though they were his friends, and it fooled them into being friendly in return. I was nothing like him in those days, scowling at the world through half-closed eyes, dazzled by the light and desperate to get back home. I was a disaster out of doors, tripping over my own shoelaces, making stupid remarks to waitresses and generally getting in the world's way. I was happy for my father, but I could never become him. Anyway, as I was saying, I used to watch him get into the taxi every morning – it was an event to me back then, seeing the car pull in, that herald of the dawn with its luminous white headlights and nameless driver.

I want you to tell you all about what happened to me the day after the spat with George. I'd been up all night listening to the rain on the windows and watching films. It was just getting to my favourite part of Crocodile Dundee (the bit where he walks over the heads of the commuters in the Subway to get to his true love) when I heard Dad tramping downstairs to get dressed. I felt a rush of adrenaline flood through me at the sound of his footsteps, knowing something was different about this morning but unable to figure out why. A few times in my life previous to this morning I had experienced the same sensation, and usually ended up doing something stupid as a result of it. The first time I had asked a girl in my class if she would be my girlfriend. She had sniggered, as seven year olds do, and agreed, only to roundly ignore me for the next two years, going so far as to take another boyfriend in my stead without having the common decency to break up with me properly. The second time, I had stood up on a bus and asked a bully to stop pulling my hair. He had continued to do so, of course, and it wasn't long after this incident that a third rush of adrenaline inspired me to ask Mother if I could drop out of school altogether. She had been relieved at this decision, and the rushes of adrenaline had stopped shortly afterwards – that was, until now. It was a mesmerising sensation – to feel compelled to move after a lifetime of inaction, and before I knew it I was out of bed and standing in the living room.

"Father, please don't telephone for a taxi today, I'll gladly drive you to the station!" I said, lowering my voice so as not to wake George.

"You'll gladly do what now?" Dad asked. "Speak like you live in this century would you? Life's too short!"

"I can hardly help the way I speak," I said.

"Like hell you can't – you're just like your mother… you put that accent on to make yourself sound su… superior." It was then that I realised he was still drunk.

"Sit there Dad, I'll go get dressed and drive you to the station," I said, as if it were the most natural thing in the world to do.

When I re-entered my bedroom, it suddenly looked different to me. This wasn't the room of someone who was sticking around forever - it was a stop-off point for refuelling and refreshing before venturing out into the real world. I had a stockpile of unopened Christmas and birthday presents in the corner of my room dating back to 2009, and I picked a t-shirt shaped one and tore the paper open. It was a simple white t-shirt with long sleeves and the fabric had a sensual texture to it which I found rather stimulating. I unwrapped the wallet George bought me back in 2010, shoved my life's savings in it and stuck it in my back pocket. Then, I brushed my hair until it shone, pulled on a brand new pair of birthday socks and braced myself for adventure.

It was a wonderful feeling to open the door and step outside at last, and as I strode out toward Dad's Mercedes I felt like crying with pride. It was a very expensive car which he'd bought from the company he worked for when he got promoted, and I'd only driven it once before, right after passing my test. Dad was just drunk enough to let me drive it that morning, and it's only really now that I fully appreciate how lucky I was that he hadn't been sober, otherwise I would have spent the best day of my life holed up in my bedroom designing video games that nobody wanted to play. Instead, I opened the car door and sat in the driver's seat.

How magical it was, gazing through the rain-jewelled windscreen at the dancing black brambles that lined the driveway. I lived in a fantasy world even back then, and I was so excited about going out that I might as well have been venturing into space itself, on a manned mission to a distant planet. I opened the window and leaned back out of it, admiring the way the silent sky towered up into a deep blue oblivion of galaxies, imagining myself spiralling upwards and into the centre of the universe. Every now and then a bird would land on the granite, eye me suspiciously, then fly off into the darkness, and the sense of excitement I felt that it would soon be *me* whizzing off into the morning was sensational. I'd passed my driving test five years before, and driven twice since, having decided there was nowhere worth going, but as Dad closed the front door behind him, pulling his coat over his shoulders, I somehow knew that everything would be fine.

Dad flipped his collar up over his wattle and trudged toward me, one hand supporting his damaged vertebrae in anticipation of pain. It was a bitterly cold morning, and in his rush to reach the car he stepped into a sludge-filled pothole. Then he opened the car door and showed me his left leg.

"Look at that!" he said as he slung his carrier bag over into the back seat. His shoes were glistening with gravel, and a dirty halo of water was creeping up the corduroy of his trouser-leg. I said nothing, hoping to make the best out of a bad start, as the sense of excitement I'd felt was already ebbing away. I'd wanted the trip to be perfect, not a non-stop whine fest about how wet his leg was. 'You should go in and change your trousers,' the voice my mind said, testing out the phrase to see how it would sound if I said it aloud. He'd probably crack a crude joke about trousers needing to be changed, which would make me feel even more uncomfortable than I already did. Either that or he'd tell me he was 'big enough, old enough and ugly enough to make his own decisions', a phrase which he used to say so often it made me want to pounce on him in a rage whenever he said it.

Opting for silence, I put the key in the ignition, surprised at the feeling of power the little metallic click gave me. When the rolling cloud of fumes ensuing from my foot's pressure on the pedal blew forth over the bonnet and dispersed into the atmosphere, I felt like an ancient Greek god, commanding the very powers of the heavens themselves. I was finally in charge, and for a split second, it felt fantastic. Then, Dad's phone rang, and he put his hand out in front of my chest - a gesture which meant "Stop the engine while I take this call." Annoyed, I did.

"It's your mother. Here, have a listen to what I have to put up with," he said, setting it to speaker phone.

Irritating as I found her, I flinched at this betrayal of my mother's trust, instinctively leaning away from the phone in a show of protest which was lost on him.

"Complaints department, Bill speaking," he said, staring straight at me.

"Why didn't you lock the door behind you?" Mum said.

"I was drunk. I'm *still* drunk."

"I won't be spoken to in that tone, Bill. And you mustn't drive drunk!"

"Anything else? You might as well get it all off your chest."

"You didn't finish your lasagna."

"Whatever."

"No, Bill, *not* whatever." He held the phone away from his ear and toward me. I wound my window down to lean out of it, a light drizzle settling on the back of my hand. "This *isn't* about me nagging, it's about you behaving irresponsibly," she said as he held the phone in my face.

"*Here, you can have her if you like,*" he said. I was about to unbuckle my seatbelt and get out of the car altogether when he put the phone back to his ear. "Yes Mum, you were saying?"

"I said, you're the bad guy here, Bill, not me!"

"Sorry Mum…" He covered the phone and leaned toward me. "*She hates being called that…*" he said with beer on his breath. 'Can I go now Mum?"

"If you insist on behaving so terribly then, yes, you most certainly can!" she said, hanging up on him.

"She talks to me like that all the time when you're not around," he said, bending to dab the sludge from his trouser-leg.

"Indeed," I said with forced familiarity, turning the word around in my mind after I'd said it. *Indeed?* Who was I to think we could be boys together? I sounded like an idiot. *Indeed.* I turned the key in the ignition again, miserably, this time.

"My sock's all soggy and there's grit in my shoes," Dad said, fiddling with his foot as I stepped down hard on the gas and let the car glide out of the tree-lined drive, glad to be away from the oppressive blackness of the yard. "Remind me to take my Berghaus out the back before we leave, would you?"

The motion sickness I felt as we sped up the road was immediate, a dull, elastic ache which pulled away at my insides as I accelerated up what passed as a hill by Cranley's standards. Not long to go, but even a journey as short as this felt intolerable to me now.

As I drove along, however, I found that the dark and stormy flatlands of the Suffolk countryside had a soothing effect upon my psyche, and I began to relax as the endless black fields spotted with hedges, swans and puddles spooled out beside me, like a dull roll of patterned satin unwinding. It was a dark, enchanting kind of beauty, and as the car soared through it like a phantom I imagined we were escaping some great apocalyptic disaster, fleeing the hurricanes and house fires that signaled the end of the world. Dad's silence allowed me the luxury of imagining such things, and I drove along in this trance for a full three minutes before wondering if I ought to break the silence for the sake of politeness.

"Looks like it might rain all day from the looks of it," I said, trying to sound a bit more common for him. It was an addle-minded sentence that made little sense, and when no reply came, I gazed out at the road, hating myself for having said it. The horizon whizzed past, flat and black against a bright orange sky from which one dark cloud after another released a fine haze of rain. Then, the world became touched with white – masses of shadow gently revealing themselves as nettles, shrubs and hedges as the light hit them, one branch at a time.

Unfortunately, this bliss couldn't last - Dad's silence was beginning to stress me out, and I desperately searched my memory for something to say that would engage his interest.

"Oh, goodness me, you don't get views like this in the… the big cities, eh?" I said. "There are… there are derelict estates everywhere you look, and crime on the streets. Give me the good old countryside any day of the week." (I was talking nonsense, you understand.) "I wonder why they do it, I mean live in the city and all of that. It's sad, very sad!"

"What *are* you harping on about?" he said. "Look. I don't suppose I could borrow your socks once we get to the station could I, Alex? It's just that you don't have

37

anywhere else to go after this and I'd be a lot happier at work today if my feet were dry."

"Sure, no problem," I heard myself say, unable to believe he would actually put me through this indignity when the time came. His suggestion was a peace offering - an apology for his distant treatment of me. It meant family, intimacy and friendship – anything but that when we got to the station he was actually expecting me to wear his wet socks. I decided to change the subject.

"Didn't you say you grew up in a council house, Dad?" I said.

"Oh, yes."

"Oh," I said, giving him time to expand on this further. He didn't. "So it was a nice house then?"

"Not really, it was a prefab. Rotten little shack in the middle of Ipswich."

"And you lived there until Grandad saved up enough…" I said, pausing in order to tease this all too familiar story out of him.

"That's right, saved up enough to buy the cottage we live in today. Shows you what you can do if you're careful with your money. You'll find that out for yourself if you ever get a job."

This was a low blow, and he fell silent after delivering it, giving me ample time to reflect upon the hopelessness of my life. I was nothing compared to Dad – a mere zero. I stopped the car at a T junction and listened to the regular tick of the indicator, thinking about what a pristine sound it made - so reliable, so simple. Dad understood every mechanism in the car down to the last detail - and his knowledge wasn't just limited to that - he had so much to give to the world, had he found a place in it which was all his own. Meanwhile there was me, still coming to terms with the fact that I actually existed, that whether I felt liked it or not, I always had to be somewhere, *doing something.*

"I was working two jobs when I inherited that house, and I still found the time to fix it up somehow," Dad said suddenly, as though someone had just pressed his 'on' switch. "I scythed the meadow, planted veg, built chicken coops, made sheds, painted walls. You name it, I did it - all after coming back from work too. Take that pond of ours you're so fond of gazing into – I dug that with my bare hands after a double-shift, for god's sake, that's how resilient I was at your age. Never hired workmen for stupid amounts of money either. No, I could do it all myself. Good *god* you take after your mother."

"I don't know how you did it," I said, feeling bitterly hurt that he'd pounced on the opportunity to attack me so quickly.

I overtook the hedge trimming vehicle that trundled along ahead of us and noticed that the driver was a woman.

"Don't suppose you noticed, but it was a woman driving that thing back there," I said, thinking it was the kind of thing he might like to talk about.

"Your mum helped with the garden too, of course. I was lucky to have her back then, she was a saint!"

"Really?" I asked, waiting for him to continue, and then, "What kind of things did she used to do?"

"She used to pick lavender and make little scented cushions for old ladies. She could have made a business out of it if she'd wanted to. Good days those were. Then she got pregnant with you and that was it. End of story. Finito."

I glanced over and saw him wipe tears from his tired, yellowed eyes.

"Yeah, sorry about that," I said. "So do you think you'll need that jacket today after all?"

Dad's phone rang before he could reply. "Listen to this," he said, putting it on speakerphone. "Yes?"

"Please tell me you didn't eat George's oat biscuits for breakfast after the fuss last night?"

"*What fuss last night?*"

"Don't pretend you were too drunk to remember, Bill. You'll have to buy some more before he notices."

"Blah, blah, blah. Can we fast-forward to the bit where I say sorry?"

"Don't give me that cheek, Bill, I'm sick of it!"

"Is there anything else Milady desires? Bonbons from Paris? Olives from Spain? No - just the biscuits, eh? No reply? Allow me to summarise – you said you were mad, I said I was sorry, you're speechless with happiness and things are back to normal. Okay, have a nice day, dear."

Dad hung up.

"It's a full-time job dealing with that one, I tell you," he said. There was a long silence after that, which was finally broken by my father saying "Have you ever *tried* women, son?"

I pulled to a halt at the traffic lights, pretending I hadn't heard him, but the question cut me to the quick. How the hell was I supposed to have *tried* women? Or *men* for that matter? For god's sake, I'd never tried anything at *all*, and what's more, Dad knew it, unless of course he meant the time I saw my cousin Kirsty in her pyjamas when she slept over at ours due to her house setting on fire, but Mum had refused to let her stay another night after that and I never saw her again.

I looked out at the village while I waited for the lights to change, wondering why Dad refused to speak to me about a single subject I had any knowledge of. A young girl wearing headphones was jogging past the bus on my left, for example – now, if Dad could have taken take his eyes off his mobile phone for a moment, we could have had a conversation about how the electricity in her headphones converted itself into sound. *That* was the kind of conversation I wanted to have with him, not this nonsense about relationships and people skills. I was pretty sure of our geographical co-ordinates at this stage – from the position of the sun in the sky I could more or less tell that we were facing due north. Why not chat about this?

"We're facing due north, right?" I asked him – and when he didn't respond I said, "Do you have a compass on this car?"

41

"No. I usually have one on my watch, but I'm wearing my Citizen Eco-Drive today," he said.

"Well, we're facing due north. You can tell from the sun."

"Hmm. Good, good."

"Dad?"

"Hmm?"

"How much petrol do you think the bus in front of us would need to consume in order to drive to Ipswich bus station from that exact spot on the road if it continued at precisely its current speed?"

"Alex, what *planet* are you from?" This unnecessary question wormed into my brain for the next few minutes, nibbling away at it from the inside until I felt as though I might have a panic attack right there at the wheel, but Dad wasn't finished with me yet.

"Talking to you is like taking my exams all over again!" he continued, determined to keep going until I had a total nervous breakdown. "You should get out more - meet women, eat ice-cream, I don't bloody know. *How much petrol do you think...* Honestly! I had two kids and a mortgage at your age! I didn't have the time or energy to think about... bloody... petrol!"

Those were his exact words. He was drunk, of course, and I tried to keep this fact in mind as I drove, unable to think of a response to his statement. I needn't have bothered, of course – Dad had clearly moved on, and was busy making a text message on his phone. I concentrated on the road as we passed through the town in order to center myself again. Tints of colour had begun to emerge from the gloom, and it was as if the rain itself were infused with light, brightening everything it fell upon. A thrill fluttered through my heart at the sight of the world waking up. A shop light flickered on, a window cleaner set up his ladder, a litter-picker in a luminous vest stooped down over something disgusting. Curiosity flooded through me. Why did people do these things when they ought to be in bed? It certainly couldn't be to make a living – if one was determined to earn a crust, the stock market was the obvious choice. They had to be hobbies – it was the only explanation. How lucky they were to be paid for something they so enjoyed! Meanwhile, I did nothing. Sitting in my room designing videogames that nobody wanted to play. I looked over at Father and wished he would say something comforting. Instead, he laughed awkwardly and proceeded to read out the text message he'd just received.

"No excuse for hanging up on me," he said, "Don't forget the biscuits. Oh *bugger off* Margaret! Why doesn't she ask *you* to buy them, eh? She knows I'm going to work today. Probably thinks you're too scared to go into a shop on your own, that's why. Well, I can't be bothered with this anymore. Is it too much to ask to be left alone for a while?"

"Nope," I said.

"You lot won't be content 'till I'm six feet under." Dad rolled his scarf into a ball and used it as a pillow, lodging it in the crook of his neck. "I don't know," he said, taking off his glasses and massaging the bridge of his nose. "Maybe *I* won't either." He closed his eyes.

Morning's on its way. There seems to be no way of stopping it except going to bed and pulling the covers over this whole sorry business. But what if I don't *want* the sun to rise? I mean, with all my heart and soul don't want it to? When I was younger I went through a phase of thinking I was a vampire. I *despise* the light unless it contrasts with shade. A warm, yellow sliver of sun on a shadow-black carpet is a lovely thing to look at, but open the door to a wide golden glow and it just hurts too much. I can't explain it.

The sun this morning is a pale one, glowing opalescent through the dust-frosted glass, and if it wasn't for the sound of the rain outside I might not be able to cope with this alone. Luckily, the hiss and sparkle of it is company enough to keep me focused on my task. I've just finished emptying the walk-in cupboard, where I found, among bags full of shoes, gadgets, trinkets and biscuit tins, a brick-fat stack of train tickets, bound up by a red rubber band. Dad used to keep these for his accountant so he could claim his train fares through his expense account, and looking through the pile, it occurred to me that one of those tickets might once have been mine. It would take me a lifetime to figure out which, but it's in there somewhere.

The few moments of peace Dad had managed to snatch in the time it took me to drive from the roundabout to the station seemed to have done him good, and he gave me a strange half smile as he unbuckled his seat belt, about to get out of the car.

"Give me those socks would you, I'm in a rush," he said, and without a second thought, I took off my shoes, pulled the warm, soft socks from my feet and handed them to him. In return he gave me his – as limp and wet as a couple of mackerel skins, and said "Righty-ho, don't do anything I wouldn't do," before getting out of the car and slamming the door behind him without another word. I watched him walk away.

The socks were even more wet and disgusting than I imagined they'd be, but there was something strangely soothing about the intimacy of the act. *We must really be good friends* I thought to myself, wiggling my feet into them. As I cast my father a final glance, I noticed a little pink patch of skin on the back of his pate. Maybe it was just the way the light was shining onto his hair, but I'd never really noticed it before and it made me feel very sorry for him. I started the engine and put the car into gear, before flinching at the feel of an unfamiliar object beneath my fingers. It was Dad's glasses, wedged next to the gear stick. He couldn't see far without them, despite his boasts of 20/20 vision, and I realized if I didn't take them to him, he'd be wandering around half blind for the rest of the day.

I felt a sudden rush of adrenaline surge through me once more. It was telling me I wasn't going to drive home as planned. Instead, it bade me, I would get out of the car and give him his glasses. Not a huge decision in itself, but it meant walking out in the street, being noticed, being part of things, if only for a moment. I couldn't decide whether or not I wanted to do it, and sat, frozen with indecision for a few minutes, waiting for a sign. Then, glancing at the back seat, I saw it. The bag containing his brand new jacket.

I'd been desperate to try the Berghaus on since the moment I saw it last night, and here I was, sitting in the car dressed in nothing but a long-sleeved t-shirt and jeans. Now wouldn't it make sense if I borrowed his coat to go out in the rain to give him his glasses? I reached over and caressed the smooth orange fabric, then pulled it out of the bag entirely and put it on, savoring the hushed rustle of the fabric and that brand-new synthetic smell. I put his glasses in one of the zip-up pockets, got out of the car and marched across the car park, avoiding the puddles along the way.

After just a few minutes of exposure to the rain my lustrous hair began to tangle, but the jacket gave me confidence, and I went up the steps, peering around the corner. I saw Dad straight away. It was a heart-rending sight. The damp patch from the puddle had spread up his trouser-leg a little more, and he was trying to scratch it with his foot and losing his balance. Finally, he gave up and sat on a bench, trying to dab the water out of the fabric with his scarf. I unzipped the pocket and took out the glasses, but I didn't go over and give them to him. I was enjoying wearing the jacket very much, and besides, he didn't need them just yet.

Despite the freshening effect of the rain, the smell of the platform utterly disgusted me. The last time I'd stood on one I'd been twenty-four years old, eating a forbidden 'Just Juice' ice lolly which Father had given me a pound to buy despite Mother's best efforts to restrain him. Filled with nostalgia, I wanted more than anything in the world to run over and give him a hug for his selflessness. Instead, I continued to watch him until the train came into view on the horizon – knowing that if I didn't give him the glasses soon it would be too late.

The turquoise East Anglian train slid toward us. It had been a decade since I had seen a train in real life and I couldn't help but notice how beautiful its red and yellow stripes were as it hissed to a halt. Dad was halfway up the platform ready to get on, and as people leaned out of the open windows ready to open the door-handles, I happened to catch the eye of a very attractive woman. I stared at her as though she were a goddess, and as she walked past me I was overwhelmed by the sweet citrus scent of her perfume, which drifted by me like an enchanted mist.

'Shall I compare thee to a summer's day?' The line of the poem I'd memorised as a child popped into my head. If it ever applied to anyone, it was to her – she smelt of ripe summer fruits, exuding warmth and promise. I watched her walk away for a few moments, wondering if I should go and speak to her, perhaps even recite the poem to her. I wondered for too long, however, and when I cast a glance back up at the platform I saw my Dad was about to board his carriage.

"Either get on the train or step away from the platform edge!" the guard shouted. Horrified, I realised he was addressing me. Faced with such a stark choice, and sensing from the tone of his voice that he would prefer me to do the former, I stepped forward, and before I knew what was happening, the doors closed behind me, the engine started, and the train gathered speed. Not long ago I had been perched on the end of my bed in my pyjamas, close to tears. Now here I was, standing on a moving train, like Bruce Willis in 'Die Hard with a Vengeance'.

Strangely, I experienced no sense of panic as we pulled out of the station. In fact, it was a wonderful thrill. I was safe with Dad on the next carriage, he wouldn't let anything happen to me. I watched him from the vestibule and when I was sure he hadn't seen me, sat down two seats behind him, angling myself so I could see his reflection in the window.

The situation inside the carriage was curious, because everyone seemed so at home in each other's company despite the fact that they had clearly never met each other. A petite woman in an oversized coat slumbered in the end seat, her two children slouched at either side of her, playing games on their mobile phones. If I had Dad's money, I might seriously have considered finding out whether the father was still an issue, and if not, introducing myself to her when she awoke. She looked worn out, but given some fancy American make-up and tailored clothes she might be a lovely little wife to me one day. I could look after the children no problem – I'd hire a nanny to tend to them while I went to Japan with their mother. Of course that all sounds a little sexist when you write it down, but if you're a destitute woman in a tight spot who happens to meet a man like that, I'm sure it's a different story.

In the film 'Pretty Woman' Julia Roberts changes her tune completely when she realizes how rich Mr. Gere is, and he was at least ten years my senior in that film from the looks of him. My hair had started to thin slightly even back then, but there was hardly a grey hair on me and I looked after myself too, eating gluten free, vegan foods wherever possible. As for more personal matters - well, I don't mean to sound judgmental, but she could have caught anything off Richard Gere's character, the way he conducted himself, whilst I, on the other hand, was a pristine virgin! Of course, I hadn't any money apart from what was in my wallet, but that was the only advantage he had over me. I was a swarthy young man in the prime of my life, why wouldn't Julia want me?

48

When I looked back at Dad he was skim-reading the Metro magazine. He couldn't care less about reading the news, of course – when he had a hangover all he liked to do was sleep. Not me. I was full of beans and ready to conquer the world that day. I only wished I had brought an umbrella, as a cursory glance at my reflection showed that my long, ash-blond locks had begun to knot at the ends from the rain, and my bald spot was beginning to show where the roots of my hair had clumped together with water.

As the train sped up, I felt the pulp of last night's lasagna move about inside my stomach, and I peered out of the window to stave off the motion sickness. I thought about the Mercedes, still parked at the station, and what my mother would say if she knew what I was doing. What a *thrill*. The countryside was brighter now through the blur of rain, revealing toy buildings whose miniature back-gardens were dotted with swings and trampolines. It was a strange feeling, whizzing past so many homes at such a high speed – I felt like Superman, and as each house turned and nodded from behind the windowpane, I started to feel as though the world was acknowledging my existence at last.

As we went through a tunnel, I got a good look at Dad's reflection - it was the face of a phantom vanishing into the abyss. Perhaps he put an act on when he was around me. The thought of this was fascinating, as he always seemed to have such an easy way with people.

After scrabbling about in his suitcase for a while, he took out a notebook and a pen. Turning to a new page, he swept his palm across the paper, testing his pen on its surface. I watched him with fascination, every muscle in my body tense at the thought that he might look up and see me.

I was absolutely scandalized at what happened next. A woman came into our carriage, and when Dad noticed she was struggling to put her bags in the overhead luggage rack, he stood to help, despite the obvious pain this caused him. I slouched down in my seat and watched him smile at the woman in a way I had never seen him look at my mother, wondering what on earth Mum would think if she could see what he was up to. Strangely enough, however, I found myself rooting for him. I was always a sucker for a good romance, and the fact that it involved my dad made it a forbidden one, which was *even better*. Dad sat back down and stared out of the window, glancing at the woman's reflection and trying to meet her gaze.

If only she had sat next to me instead! I was a free agent, and when I say free I mean completely untouched. For the second time that morning, I found myself wanting to recite Sonnet 18 out loud. Ah, it was heartbreakingly lovely, and to perform it for her on a train would be the height of romance. I had spent some effort memorizing the entire sonnet as a boy of ten, hoping to recite it to a certain dark-haired girl at a disco the local youth club was having. I had first noticed her in Sunday school after her mother told her not to talk to me, and had been smitten with her for months. The sonnet had taken me a long time to learn, but it had been worth it, and if my mother hadn't forbidden me from going to the disco that day, I believe I might have a romance story or two of my own to write about, not to mention a couple of kids by now! All through my youth, Mother had indulged in the habit of falling sick whenever we were supposed to be going out – of suddenly feeling faint when I needed to be driven to a party, or throwing a tantrum when someone tried to speak to me directly. She seemed to have an extreme allergy to the idea of my having a life, and the easiest option for me was to pander to this unquestioningly. No doubt if she had known I was on a train that day, despite my being thirty-four years old at the time, she would have died with her leg up. She liked to have me around the house in case George got funny with her, you see.

"What's your name, then?" Dad asked the woman, just like that.

"Erm… Kate."

"Kate is it? Lovely name," he said, leaning forward. "You know, I've never met a Kate I didn't get on with. Met a lot of them too, I was meeting Kates before you even *became* one, no doubt. How old are you? Let's see… I'd say about 23, am I right? Course I'm right, I saw it on your rail-card. Eyes like a hawk, this one! Guess my age. Go on! What do you think?"

"I dunno, about 79?" she said, looking around for other seats. I recoiled from her gaze in horror in case she drew Dad's attention to me.

"I'm 65," he frowned. "Now, if I was 64 we wouldn't be having this conversation."

"Oh, a conversation - is that what this is?"

"I wouldn't have tried to chat up a complete stranger last year. That's because I still had something left to live for… Guess what I've got now?" Dad's voice began to crack. "*Sod all*, pardon my French, that's why I'm writing *this*!"

He tore a page from his diary and slapped it down on the table for her to read. I had no idea what he might have written on it, but it was clear that the woman wasn't impressed. She took a look at it and said "Do I look like a counsellor to you?" before taking a pair of headphones from her handbag and plugging them into her mobile phone.

What if it was a suicide note? Dad's greatest fear was that he was going to die in a nursing home, and he knew not to expect special treatment if he became dependent upon us. George had always made it clear to Mum and Dad that he had no intention of caring for them in their old age, and it would be unfair on me if I were to take on the whole burden of caring for them myself. Dad wouldn't stand a chance if left in my hands, anyway - why, he would be little more than a pet to me, left slouched on the sofa for days. I knew this from experience. Once, he was sick for a whole month while Mum went to Peru to 'find herself'. It was an infectious illness, and not wanting to expose ourselves to it, we left him in the recovery position on the parlor couch for a week and hoped for the best.

Oh, it was hell in that house without Mother! One day while Dad was asleep, I noticed a smell coming from the chimney. Well, it turned out there was a dead pigeon stuck up there, but of course, without her being around to dislodge it the whole house started to smell unbearable. After a week, I decided to leave the front door open to diffuse the smell, but this allowed a hideous tide of spiders, midges and mice to creep into all the warm corners of the living room. No doubt all of this would have been symbolic if it wasn't such a commonplace sight in our house. You have to have a tough disposition to live out in the middle of the country with all the wee beasties. Of course, something had to be done about it eventually, and I knocked it down with a broom handle after much kerfuffle. I was unable to look at the corpse, throwing a towel over it for Mother to deal with when she came back home (there was no point expecting George to do it). When Mother finally returned, George made her swear she would never leave the house again, and she agreed. Perhaps that was the reason she never divorced Dad – he was more or less the only man she had the opportunity to speak with apart from her sons. Dad, on the other hand, seemed to have taken his chances with women whenever he got them, if his little performance on the train that day was anything to go by.

"Ladies and gentleman, we will soon be arriving at our final stop, Ipswich, that's Ipswich, your last station stop. Please make sure you have collected your belongings before leaving the train, and mind the gap between the train and platform edge."

Dad stood up straight away, obviously embarrassed at having shared his deepest secrets with someone who couldn't care less.

It would be dreadful if he decided to kill himself. How would we survive? Mother wouldn't be able to cope on her own. I imagined the rest of our lives without him - unopened bills piling up on the kitchen table, waist-high weeds encasing the house, weaving their warp and weft through the fence, around the trees, until the cottage was encased in a suffocating wilderness. Oh, the horror of letting in thoughts like these – images that had cast their shadows against the otherwise pristine wall of my subconscious since the moment I first learnt of the existence of poverty. Now, the stark possibility of it was seeping into every atom of my being, haunting me from within. A lifetime without money. Fish finger sandwiches, scratch cards on the mantelpiece and coupons at the supermarket till. The thought of it was too much to bear. I had to stop him!

As I stepped off the train, a rush of cool air hit my face and I marveled at the whiteness of the outside world. A fine drizzle was falling from a sky so blank it seemed cloudless, and as I watched my father walk down the station steps, grasping at the bannister like a blind man, it suddenly occurred to me that he wasn't going to work after all, as he had come right into Ipswich instead of getting off the train at Needham Market. What if he meant to kill himself today? Worse still, what if he was headed for the job centre? The letter he showed the woman could have easily been one of resignation. I chased the latter thought out of my head before it drove me mad.

I followed Dad out of the station and saw him leaning against a wall, blinking into the mid distance with a puzzled expression on his face. There was something about the temperature of the air, the quality of the light, the exact colour of the tarmac beneath his feet, which made the image of him so tragic that it was difficult not to run to him and beg him to come back home. Indeed, if I hadn't have been wearing his jacket, I might have done it.

Chapter Three

Poor Father! I felt terrible for him. Still, it was wonderful to actually *feel* something for a change. This didn't just feel like grief - it felt like joy, like love, like the first few years of being alive. What if it had indeed been a suicide note? I wondered what it would be like to die, imagining myself released on that deep violet tide which glimmered so irresistibly on the horizon. I closed my eyes. The freedom to become *nothing* – it was something I had secretly craved for years – the choice to keep my eyes closed until the end of time, though the sun shone and the world rolled by outside. For years I had walked through the cold of it, suffered a hundred needless blows with my open palms upturned. I opened my eyes and looked for my father, and as I walked toward him I felt as though I were sinking deeper and deeper into the chasm of myself, overwhelmed with the desire to disappear.

He was only fifty paces away, but what a difference that distance made! I held his glasses in my hand, steeling myself to give them to him. He kept gazing up at the rows of unfinished apartments in the distance, probably only now realising he would never see his own home again. He started to swing his briefcase about, and it suddenly occurred to me that it might be empty – that he was "doing a Douglas", so to speak. Then he disappeared into a building. He was in there a while, and as I waited, I looked in the shop windows at the various arrangements of rings, watches, iPads, shoes and handbags that gleamed out from one halogen-lit display after another. Being able to afford them, I could be absolutely certain that I didn't want them. How quickly that might change one day! I was about to head toward Dad when a woman with a strangely bohemian look approached me. She had a scarf wrapped around her head, and was holding a stack of magazines.

"Please sir, Big Issue, sir?" she said. I was taken aback by this. To be approached in the middle of the street by a chic European woman was a dream come true for me. She was one of the only young ladies on the street who seemed at all concerned enough by the signs of the approaching storm to wear a waterproof jacket. It was hardly a Berghaus, but it was a sign of good sense, and I felt sure that here, indeed, was a woman whose priorities in life matched mine.

"What's this?" I asked her, taking one of the magazines she held out to me. It was clearly a literary publication of some sort. "Are you the editor?"

"Please sir. You buy?" I was half in love with her already at this point, and whilst impressed at the depth of her commitment to the publication, I didn't have any pound coins, and the wait for change would have been excruciatingly embarrassing.

"How much?" I asked, as the smile began to sink from her face.

"Only £2.50, sir."

"Well, you ought to charge more," I said. "Do you understand me?" She frowned. "This magazine is too cheap! You… will… never… make… a… profit!"

She shook her head at me, and I realised I had offended her. Of course, she wasn't doing it for the money and it had been tactless for me to suggest as much. The gentlemanly thing to do was to walk away.

"Thank you sir, hope you have a lovely day," she said, rather sadly.

I turned back to look at her as I walked by, wishing I had done things differently. Over the course of a minute and a half, this incredible woman had treated me with more kindness and respect than I had received in the last few decades from my own mother, and here I was, walking away from her like an idiot. I had just about made my mind up to go back to her when she started speaking to someone else. Of course – how stupid of me. She was a popular woman with no shortage of people to talk to. Still, she must have seen something in me that spoke of an intellectual, and I found solace in this as I walked away.

The woman had shone like a beacon of culture and civility in an otherwise heathen world, and upon leaving her company I was even more shocked at the poverty all around me than ever. What would my life have been like, I wondered, if my parents had let me wander around Ipswich city centre on my own like a scoundrel? I was grateful to Mother for sparing me that misery at least. I couldn't have lived in Ipswich to save my life - the one or two refined features of the place were few and far between, although I very much enjoyed the quaint little market stalls, with their dainty little fairy lights and blue and white striped tarpaulins.

Still, there was something too tacky for words about the place. I followed Dad further into the market, and was passing by one of the stalls when a man in costume shouted directly in my ear.

"Bana-anas, get your bana-nas, fifty pence a bunch!"

Whilst I didn't appreciate being accosted at such close quarters, the man had affected the most incredible working class accent for his performance, and there was a sonorous quality to his voice which Enrico Caruso himself would have been proud to possess.

"Bana-anas, fifty pence a bunch," he continued to shout. I felt around for a twenty pence in my pocket to give him as a token of my support, feeling rather frustrated at the knowledge that no such sum of money was close to hand. This was the second time today I had understood the importance of small change, and I realised that to never break a five pound note was to cut oneself off entirely from an essential part of the human experience – the joy of giving.

"Bana-anas, fifty pence a bunch!" he cried again, and having found nothing in my pockets, I started applauding loudly, hoping some of the old ladies standing behind me with sour looks on their faces would join in to offer him their support.

"Get out of the way, you bloody nutter," one of them said, shouldering past me and offering the fellow her money impatiently.

Horrified at the way she had spoken to me, I apologised and darted out of her way. The worst part of this whole affair, however was not the woman's unkindness, but the way the man glared at me as I stepped away from him. It was as though I had somehow robbed the fellow of something vitally important! This is one of the reasons I have such little time for artists. I'm a very sensitive person myself but would never 'put myself out there' if I couldn't handle such little mishaps.

The longer I watched people walk past, the harder it was to care what they thought about me. The poverty of the place was beginning to overwhelm me. Everywhere I looked there were people suffering - pensioners eating pasties out of greasy paper packets, babies getting dirty dummies stuck back into their mouths, and underfed wretches of all ages limping about and smoking cigarettes. Meanwhile, Dad had emerged from the shop carrying a plastic bag. He sat on a wall and rummaged through it, rubbing his eyes. Remembering that he probably couldn't see a thing without his glasses I ventured nearer and saw that he had bought a six pack of beer. Not only that, but he was getting ready to drink one right there in the street, just as though he were one of *them*. How exciting, and wouldn't Mother be furious?

Only a man on the edge drinks beer on the street, I told myself, thinking once again that perhaps he was planning to kill himself. I thought about the last things *I* might choose to do if I were about to commit suicide – drink a beer or two in the privacy of my own home? Certainly. Dare myself to smoke a pack of cigarettes? Yes, perhaps. Anything but chug down on a beer in this poverty-stricken slum. I imagine it was his working class roots calling him back home. Was this really who he was, deep down?

He wandered along until he came to a chip van, where he rummaged around in his wallet for money, as if actually inclined to make a purchase. To my horror, he bought a tray of something disgusting, gazing at it as if waiting for some moment of clarity to hit, and then began to eat it.

His final meal, I thought to myself, miserably as I followed him up the street, realising where he was headed at last.

He was bound for the Marina – perhaps he had decided to drown himself there, before the food poisoning set in.

The gothic cranes, abandoned scaffolds and broken windows loomed above his diminutive figure. It's worth noting that Dad was consistently one of the best dressed individuals on the street that day. He was wearing a jolly expensive suit too - £800 it cost, hand-tailored in Jermyn Street. I know this, because I went to the tailors with him while he got fitted for it. He wanted to show me the perks of having a job, you see, and while he was choosing his tie, the assistant informed me that the specific kind of blue tweed he had chosen would have to be shipped in from two separate factories, as it was in such short supply.

Now, this little detail sticks in my mind because if he'd have ordered a two piece suit they would have been able to make it for him in no time at all, but he insisted on the waistcoat, which meant he would have to wait a whole month before it was ready. Dad didn't do things by halves, and he wanted the three piece suit so he could keep his solid gold pocket watch on him at all times. Mum never did forgive him for buying that watch.

After polishing off the last scrap of whatever culinary abomination had previously lain upon the polystyrene tray, Dad disappeared around a corner and I almost had to *run* to catch up to him. When I found him, he was staring up at a glossy black building. I mean, really staring - he stood there for five minutes or so, long enough for me to wonder what the hell was going on in his mind. He was necking his beer with an air of desperation and pressing his fingertips to the glass. Of course, now I know that this was the Willis Building, and that he'd been looking at the reflection of old civil hall that stood opposite in its vast glass panes. To this day I don't understand why he did this - the civil hall was the place he'd married my mother, but I can't imagine that this had anything to do with it, to say how much they clearly despised each other.

He was headed down Princes Street now, and I shuddered at the sight of its bleak, abandoned shops painted in dirty primary colours, envisioning the thieves and gangsters who could be lurking in the shadows beyond those dusty windows, just waiting for a well-dressed gentleman like myself to wander past.

The second stories of the shops were dull brick blocks, as flimsy as a set from an old western, and I started to imagine the horrific criminal acts which might take place up there behind those smoke-tinged net curtains. What on earth was Dad doing here? I was about to find out.

To my absolute horror, he crossed the road and stood outside Ladbrokes, looking at the posters in the window. *You wouldn't dare!* I thought to myself. *You wouldn't dare!* As if accepting my challenge, he drained the last dregs of his beer, then chucked the crumpled tin onto the street and went in.

I stood outside for a long while, gazing at the rusty old cars that were parked at careless angles outside the curved façade and wondering what on earth had inspired my father, a *Mercedes* driver, to set foot in that rotten little dive. It's not as if we needed the money. Or did we? What if he really had lost his job? It suddenly occurred to me that he might be about to gamble away my inheritance, and the more I thought about it, the more sense it made. Perhaps he was hoping that if he won, he wouldn't have to kill himself, but to me it wasn't worth the risk and I felt

61

a rush of adrenaline (my third that day) building up inside me as I determined to go inside and stop him from doing it.

I crossed the road and opened the door as quietly as I could. Nothing could have prepared me for the utter squalor of the interior. The smell of sweat permeated the room, and the filthy cream walls were covered with dog-eared posters advertising greyhounds, football, and lotto.

"The numbers are as follows," I heard someone say, "Thirty-one, thirty-eight, and forty..."

Several miserable little men populated the room, hunched over wood-effect tables with magic markers in their hands. My dad cut a fine figure in his suit as he traversed the obstacles on the gum-studded carpet, heading toward an old man who was drinking from a corrugated cup.

"How do you place a bet these days anyway?" he yelled, leaning on the man's table as if they were old friends. "Some kind of computerised system, no doubt?"

The man spat into a tissue and wiped his mouth on his sleeve, mumbling something to Dad. Dad nodded in a sombre way, then made his way to the counter. He rested his leather briefcase on the ledge, opened it up and took out his pen. I was about to go over to stop him from making a bet when a young man directly next to Dad let out the most horrible yell, scaring me half to death.

"My odds was not three-to-one! I said two to one, didn't I, Mary? Just tell that woman you 'eard me!" His way of speaking was infinitely more common than I have just made out, but I think an accurate recreation of his pronunciation would require the skills of a far more talented linguist than myself.

Meanwhile, Dad tucked his pen into his top pocket and turned slowly around, but I saw that his hand was shaking, as if he was psyching himself up to do something stupid. The woman this loud-mouthed oaf was with kept quiet. I can't remember what she was wearing, but I do know she was dressed as if she had randomly shoplifted her outfit from a charity-shop – a look which seemed to be all the rage in these parts.

The film 'Pretty Woman' came to mind again. I had £300 in my wallet, which would have paid for a fine day out for this girl had she not decided to attach herself to this incorrigible ruffian. I could have bought her a suit of clothes to be worn to a job interview, for example, or enrolled her on a food hygiene course. No doubt the girl was unemployed, and the only lucky breaks she could expect to receive in life were a pound on the lottery or a kind nod from a stranger here and there. These, I would have been happy to provide for her if I thought it would further my chances. I imagined she would look grand in a smart trouser suit with properly brushed hair, and envied her common companion his good fortune, wondering what *he* had that *I* didn't as he paced about the place, yelling like a lunatic.

To my surprise, the cashier, a pudgy teen with tired eyes and a mousy ponytail, was completely unshaken at this idiot's behaviour. I ventured closer to Dad now, trying to figure out how to stop him from placing a bet without humiliating myself in front of everyone. Dad passed his slip to the girl.

"What's the price on this?"

"This is *red* ink," she said, as though she were answering his question. Dad leaned up to the glass and lowered his voice to a mock-conspiratorial whisper.

"Is that some kind of code or what?"

"No - this is red ink, you can't write in red ink on a betting slip."

"Since when?" he cried in outrage.

"I dunno - forever."

"You see, your... your idea of forever isn't very long for me at all," he sighed, leaning on the counter. "I was knocking... knocking... I was knocking about these kinds of places for nigh on twenty years before you were born, and we used to use red... red ink back then." He nodded and waited for her to ask him a question about his life.

She had to, surely? I thought to myself. He was looking good in his suit, certainly better than the ragtag bunch of miscreants she was used to dealing with, and despite not wanting my father to place the bet I felt compelled to draw her attention to the fact that here was a man of some sophistication, to be treated accordingly. I needn't have worried, however, as my father had it all in hand. He twiddled the pen in his fingers, tapping it on her window.

"How... how old are you?"

"What's it to you?"

"Well, isn't that a nice way to talk to a... excuse me, that's my phone," Dad squinted at the mobile phone screen for a few seconds before hammering the off button and

64

turning his attention to the cashier again. He held his pen up in the air.

"However old you are, *she*, my dear, is a lot older - she's an antique lever-fill fountain pen - Conway Stewart, and she writes exclusively… in red. Rouge Bourgogne to be pre… precise. Rouge Bourgogne you ask? What's Rouge Bourgogne? It's a very expensive colour of ink." He held the pen high. "I can't fill her up with black ink without emptying the entire lot of Rouge Bourgogne down the sink. It's not one of those monstrosities you use at school, you know."

"There are people in line behind you," she said, and I stepped back in case Dad turned around and saw me, but he was so absorbed in his story about the pen I needn't have worried.

"Yes, I'm aware of that, but what I'm trying to say is, this bugger doesn't write in black."

"There's a black pen right here," she said, passing him one.

"It's not quite the same though, is it? Oh, alright, this won't take a minute." He began to scribble on a new piece of paper with the biro, handed it to the cashier, took something from her in return and walked over to the young couple.

"Don't take it so badly. I lost ten grand in here once," he said. Now, I had heard stories to this effect from Mum but had always assumed she was lying. What if he lost again? I had no idea how it worked, but had been pretty sure it couldn't be as simple as writing on a piece of paper. Could it? There was no point asking the woman how much he had bet, and I suddenly hated myself for not being clued up enough to recognise how easy it was to do. I gave Dad about half a minute's head start, then slowly opened the door and peered out.

Dad was standing fifty yards up the street, gazing up the side of a derelict building. It was rippling with the same green plastic netting that was stretched from scaffold to scaffold all over the town. It seemed as though Ipswich was fully of ugly, unfinished structures like these, with iron poles jutting out from the walls like symmetrical nests of metal, and I hated it with the heat of a thousand suns. I turned back to Dad and saw he was headed toward the old ruins of Blackfriars Church, somewhere I remembered well from my childhood as we went for a picnic there, once. It was the funniest thing - a stray dog came running over, and mother was so afraid that she jumped up and spilt her cup of tea all down the front of her lovely sunshine-yellow blouse. Oh, she made an awful fuss – her top was soaked through, and we could see her underthings - it was very exciting!

I could remember almost every single time I'd ever left the house, because it happened so rarely. Sometimes when I was still a boy, Dad would sneak me outside while Mother cooked dinner, and take me for long walks in the field beyond the back garden – he knew all the different kinds of flowers and mushrooms and would tell me how they came to be named. He was an artist, I think – he saw things in clouds that I just couldn't... castles and exotic shores. Meanwhile, I was blank inside, absolutely nothing going on at all.

Now it seemed our roles had been reversed, and as I stood there, watching the man I most admired in the world kicking pebbles into the grass, a vicious fire ignited inside me, and I was seized with the urge to smash my fist through the first car window I walked past. Instead, I maintained my distance, watching him limp away from the rubble and up the street.

Finally, Dad reached the Marina, his limping figure dwarfed by the vast, black-roofed blocks of flats. By the time he passed the painted anchor that marked the entrance, I was starting to worry deeply about what his plans might be. If he had come here to *do it*, would I watch? I couldn't cope with this thought, and tried to take in the scenery as if observing it all through a periscope, in order to cope with the stress better – sending a painless, bodiless version of myself out to observe the scene on my behalf and figure out, rationally, what to do.

Dad was getting on to a boat, alright – that much was obvious – the question was, whose? I'd heard him and Mother arguing about his intention to go halves with his friend to buy one years before, but never dreamed he would actually go through with it. I hesitated a moment before following him onto the boardwalk, surveying the rows of bobbing yachts with a deep sense of sadness.

Absolute peace governed the place, white boats standing on ceremony as I strode past, the rows of sails on their masts fluttering in the wind like celebratory flags. Silver stacks of high rise flats stood to attention in the distance, gazing at me through unblinking windows, and I somehow felt less alone there among these inanimate objects than I had in the city surrounded by people. It felt as though the world had stopped and stood to attention at my presence. It was a feeling only money could buy.

Feeling soothed by the presence of such majesty, I strolled past the glossy black bollards and romantic white ropes, thinking about how wonderful it was to be rich. I shuddered to think that once, my father was nothing but a common ruffian without a penny to his name, and watched him proudly as he reached his boat, wiping his palms on his trouser legs and holding the rigging in order to hoist himself aboard.

I decided to wait for him to kill himself, then call for the police. It was the least I could do after he'd raised and fed me for all these years. I stood there for ten minutes or so, letting my eyes settle onto the darkly glinting line of water between the boards and the boat, constantly expecting to hear the splash as he landed. He had picked a quiet day to do it.

I took in every detail of the marina as I waited, staring at the covered hulls and tarpaulins in their sombre blues and maroons. The splash I had anticipated, however, never came. Instead, he dragged a sun lounger out onto the deck, put up an umbrella, and cracked open a beer. I was wondering whether these were the last desperate moments of a man on the edge when a suntanned woman walked past, yelling out, "Not you again, Bill! Don't you have a home to go to?"

"Oh…M… Mary, how… how are you?" Dad slurred in reply. It was only then that I realised that my father had been doing this for quite some time.

Of course, I was shocked at the thought that he had been coming here to lounge about all day while we were stuck at home, but the relief that he wasn't going to kill himself rather balanced this out, and I left the marina in high spirits. After all, Dad was rich, and if he'd really bought himself a yacht, maybe we didn't need the income from his job as much as I'd previously supposed.

It was becoming rather cool outside, and I marched out of the gate and across the road as quickly as I could. I was hungry and it was time to go home, but for some reason I didn't feel like heading to the station immediately. By the time I reached the other side of the street, the intermittent drizzle had become a fine rain, and although I now had every reason to return home, there was something about the way my dad had laid himself out on that lounger that I couldn't get over. I sat on the bench, thinking to myself that if he was able to relax and take life in his stride like that for days on end, whilst telling his unsuspecting wife and children that he was heading out to work, then surely I could give myself permission to let my hair down for just one day.

I was lost in these fleeting thoughts of freedom when a petite woman walked up and sat on the bench beside me, just as comfortably as if we lived together. She was casually dressed, with a little elfin frame, and was busily drawing her hair back into a ponytail. I glanced over at her with fascination as she took a make-up bag from her satchel and started to cover her face with various creams and powders, her fingers gently dabbing this spot and that – first her lips, then her cheeks and eyelids. I took a shine to this adorable individual straight away, and when she stood up to leave, it felt natural to do the same, following her up the tree-lined road and back into town.

This little adventure was a comforting distraction after the miserable experience I'd had so far, and despite the grey, lifeless sky and the filthiness of the streets, in my heart it felt like the very height of summer. It was as though there were some chemical in the air that signified the beginning of something wonderful, and it was all I could do to stop myself from dancing down the street behind her in gleeful celebration of my new-found love.

Of course, one has to work up to such things, and I was just building up the courage to go and talk to her when she stopped outside a building, put her mobile phone into her bag, and went in. After a brief struggle with my conscience I followed her in, only to realise I was in some kind of doctor's office. Mum and Dad never did trust doctors, and almost every illness I've ever had in my life has been effectively treated with a cup of hot orange squash, plenty of fluids and a couple of days in bed, so I was very interested to see the rituals attached to the making and keeping of 'GP' appointments. The sweet little woman was standing up by the counter speaking to the receptionist, and I stood in line behind her.

"Hello there, it's Melanie Winters to see Dr Peterson at 2.15," she said, in a disappointingly working class accent.

I gave the receptionist a friendly 'I'm with her' face and followed Ms Winters to the waiting area, sitting on the seat opposite her.

It was a tiny little waiting room with harsh fluorescent lighting, fake plants, and piles of tasteless magazines strewn all over the tables. I picked one up, intrigued by a story entitled '12 things you didn't know about Richard Gere'. *Try me*, I thought to myself, laughing out loud. I didn't even need to open the magazine to know what the 'little known facts' would be. The only question in my mind was which they would rate number one. I decided that the amateur who had researched this article would more than likely list the fact that his middle name was 'Tiffany' above the far more interesting fact that he was once married to the doe-eyed Carey Lowell, a massively under-rated actress whose supporting role in 'Sleepless in Seattle' was only barely equalled by Ms Ryan's. I was leafing through the pages to find out just how serious a publication this was, when Melanie's name was called. When the coast was clear, I ambled over to the service counter and squinted at the receptionist's name badge.

"Josie, is it?" I said.

"*Jodie*, you're nearly there," she said, rifling through her paperwork. Horrified at this needless mistake, I sat back down, entering a speechless trance of such intense numbness that I felt as though I were drifting into a dense, toxic mist from which I would emerge a mere skeleton of a man. Finally, I became aware of my surroundings again, and studied the room, trying to channel something of my father's poise and dignity into my general demeanour. I wondered if it were possible to pretend to actually *be* him, if only for the few minutes it took to actually speak to her and repair the damage I had done by mispronouncing her name so dismally.

I had grown to know my father so well, I thought, that such a thing should be possible. If he were here, instead of lounging about on a yacht, he'd notice the little things in the room that made it unique and make witty observations about them in order to break the ice with her. I decided to try it. I took a good look around the room and tried to take in every detail of it. First, I noticed that the chairs were navy blue with pine legs and arms, nailed together in threes, and I considered making a joke about 'Jake the Peg', before remembering the unfortunate conviction of Rolf Harris. I searched the walls for inspiration instead. There was a faded photographic print on the wall and after squinting at it a bit, I realised that it was a picture of Blackfriars Ruins. I knew plenty about those ruins – why, I had stood among them just a few hours since! Blackfriars Ruins. I rehearsed the two words in my mind for a while – *Blackfriars Ruins, Blackfriars Ruins,* then let my tongue take a turn, blurting out "Blackfriars Ruins, eh?"

There was no response, and a minute passed in silence before I tried again.

"Blackfriars Ruins?" I said. There was no reply, and I realised I needed to assert myself in order to be heard.

"DID YOU TAKE THIS PICTURE, JOSIE?" I shouted across the room. She must have heard me that time, but still there was no response. My palms tingled and my breath became shallow. "I see you've got a picture of Blackfriars Ruins up here," I said, feeling the words burn into my windpipe. What would Dad do if he were here? I walked to the empty counter, ringing the bell three times in order to attract her fullest attention.

"Yes, how can I help you?" Jodie said. By this time I was sweating profusely, and my hands were beginning to shake. I thrust my fists into my pockets and pushed down into the fabric to absorb some of the shock this little exchange was putting on my system.

"That picture of Blackfriars Ruins you've got on the wall there. How much do you want for it?" I said, taking my wallet from my pocket and tossing it onto the counter with a cavalier attitude.

"Oh. It's not for sale."

And they wonder why the NHS is in dire straits? My dad's voice said in my mind. I wondered if I should say this to her or whether she would think I were being rude. I tested the

72

sentence again, found it to be good, and was about to say it when she ducked under the counter to pick up something she had dropped. I ought to have trusted my instinct, I thought, determining to do whatever Dad would do from now on. I took a good long look around the room, then settled my gaze on the counter. "Those great big piles of leaflets over there, how much do they cost you to produce?" I said. "Have you ever thought about going electronic? Save the planet and all that? I could revolutionise the NHS if they brought me in." I picked up a flyer from the counter and used it as a prop. "I mean, look at this leaflet... the flaws are glaringly obvious. It doesn't make efficient use of important page space, the photograph they've chosen is terrible…"

"Well, we have a complaints and suggestions box in the corner," she said, walking into the back office. I stared at the leaflet for a while before turning my attention to a wall rack full of NHS pamphlets that was nailed on the wall beside me. 'Don't be a stress head", declared one, depicting a business man with a clock for a face.

"Don't be a stress head indeed! *What kind of a ninny thinks up this claptrap?*" I said, running my finger along the rest of them. I picked up a random stack of leaflets from a table and determined to say something witty about each one of them. "Adult Social Care - I dread… I dread to think the budget they had for this. Whatever it was I could have halved it…" I looked around after saying this as it sounded convincing, but she was still nowhere to be seen. "Look at this!" I shouted, "Meals not Morsels, Space for Yourself, Understanding Anxiety..." I fell silent and sat down again, wiping the sweat from my eyelids. When I stood up again, I did so with hesitancy, ringing the bell just once.

"No need for that, I'm just here," she said, emerging from

the back room again.

"Yes…hello…" I said, giving her a friendly wave to make myself more approachable. She seemed to be about to smile, and I took this as a sign to continue in my efforts at seduction. "I was wondering if… you'd like to… make me a cup of coffee," I asked, quietly.

"Erm, if you'd like a drink, there's a water cooler and cups over there, please just help yourself."

"I thought the whole point of this place was that *you* help *me*," I said, in classic Dad fashion.

"Pardon?"

"Well, the phrase *help yourself* in a place like this, it's just laden with irony isn't it..." It's funny, but all these years later I remember saying that so vividly. For a long time I've thought I might try to write a sitcom of my own, either that or a romantic comedy – something that gives me a chance to flex my imaginative muscles and really let loose with my powers of creative play.

Then, mustering up my courage, I went for it.

"Is there a café nearby? DON'T answer that, it's not the question I meant to ask… I was just wondering if you'd like to join me for coffee later today. Don't ask, don't get and all that."

"Oh…" she began. Not 'No', but '*Oh!*' Suddenly, the double doors opened to the sight of the young woman whom I was pretending to be accompanying. She was crying, which really made things awkward for me, because I had to act as though I was concerned for her wellbeing.

In order to give this impression I stared intently at the side of her face and followed her out of the door as she left, like the idiot that I was. I didn't even stop to say goodbye to Jodie, who might well have wished to meet me for coffee tomorrow for all I knew, but there was no chance of that happening whatsoever, now that I was following another woman out of the door without waiting for her reply.

I was so unhappy about this that I stopped following Melanie the moment I was out the door, and didn't even turn to look at her after she walked away from me. I wandered around for quite some time after that, looking into shop windows. I briefly considered going back to the Marina, but there was no point in being traumatised for life by watching one's father flirt with other women. Instead, I wandered toward the bus station, reflecting on my many achievements that day. I'd done well, there was no denying that. Driving to Ipswich, following Dad without getting caught, and asking a girl on a date without even breaking a sweat. Yes, I was feeling very pleased with myself indeed by the time I got there.

I figured that the key to my sudden reversal in fortune lay in my decision to pretend that I was my father. I knew his every mannerism - the way he laughed and asked a silly question. He was whimsical and confident, and you couldn't go wrong if you mimicked him. The bus station was the perfect place to try to chat up women, because I could just catch a bus to get away if they shouted at me, or hide in the toilets until the coast was clear.

I started out looking for pretty young ladies, but I soon realised that I would be wasting my time on them. They were on the lookout for people trying to 'pick them up' all the time, and you could tell just from the way they held themselves that they had no wish to speak to a man they hadn't been formally introduced to. I finally settled on a chubby girl who was hunched over her mobile phone with her 'hoodie' up. I was a tall fellow with long flowing locks and a healthy BMI index, and she looked like the type who would be happy enough with that. Of course, it wouldn't hurt my case one bit if she were to find out that I came from money, but I decided to allow this titbit of information to come out naturally in the course of the conversation, as I was loathe to end up stuck with one of those shallow types who is interested in a man for all the wrong reasons.

I took a seat opposite her, keeping my distance so that I could observe my surroundings and formulate some interesting metaphors and similes about the place, as Father would have done. The first thing I noticed was the way that the buses were all different colours. I mean, you never notice details like these when you look out of your bedroom window and see a random bus fly past your house. Now, sitting at the depot, I realised that this was because there were several different transport companies all using this station as a base, and I was about to go and use this as my opening gambit when a bolt of inspiration hit me. The bus shelter had so much glass in it that it almost looked like a fish tank!

As if that wasn't enough to be getting on with – I mean, the sheer poetry of it, I had also noticed something else. When I was young, you see, I had a tropical fish tank, and I used to spend hours with my face pressed against the glass, peering in through it. You could see these little rainbows if you looked through it just so, and the musky, damp smell of the fish tank was such an alien scent that when I smelt it, I was transported somewhere else. I mean *really* somewhere else, watching the undulating plant life move about in that warm, murmuring water, some place where nobody knew who I was, not even me, and my imagination used to run wild when I was sitting there watching the fish suck up those coloured pebbles and spit them back out again. It was like an out of body experience!

Anyway, the important part of this story is that I used to be crazy about collecting every different type of fish they had on sale at the shop. Mum was unhappy about this because it meant that some of the aggressive carnivores would eat the more placid fish, but as far as Dad was concerned, this was a lesson about the world that I needed to learn, and learn it I did. I had Japanese fighter fish, neon tetras, kissing gouramis (I was so jealous of those for having someone to love that I was secretly glad when one of them got eaten by a lone arowana), all kinds of fish, and looking around at the buses in that station, the final piece of the puzzle slotted into place. The buses were the same colours as tropical fish! I was so pleased with myself. I started to try to formulate the perfect poetic image, and finally came up with the following poem:

'The violet bus flashes its side,
Like a tropical fish swimming through
A concrete current,
With red lights flashing in its eyes.
Like a tropical fish swimming through
A concrete current,
The violet bus flashes its side.'

I repeated this to myself at least twenty times, mouthing the words in order to promote muscle memory for so long that even after all these years it still trips effortlessly off my tongue. I was so happy with myself that I decided to channel the high while I was still riding the wave, and telling myself over and over again that I was my dad, I took a deep breath and moved to the seat next to the girl.

77

"Excuse me, is this the bus to Halifax?" I said, leaning over to get her attention. She seemed startled and glared up at me. I immediately took the hint, and was about to stand up and walk away when she said "I certainly hope so!" and laughed! Well, I took this as a flashing green light if ever there was one, and laughed along with her for quite some time, taking the opportunity to get a longer look at her face, which was very pink and squinty in the middle.

"You know, I'm sure buses always used to be the one colour here when I was young," I continued, leaning toward her a bit more.

"Hmm?"

"Bus colours," I said. "These days you get *this* company and *that* company in competition, and so each bus is a different colour. It just so happens that the colours of the buses match the colours of tropical fish. Why, it feels like I'm sitting in an aquarium!"

"Hmm?" I wished she wouldn't say that, because it made her sound dumb.

"An aquarium! What I'm *trying to say* is that the buses are all coloured like tropical fish!"

"Oh, are they doing a special promotion?" she said. I ignored this because it didn't make any sense, and began to recite my poem before I went off her completely.

"The violet flashes fish their…" It was here that my mind went blank, and in my panic I reverted to the only poem in the world I knew.

"Shall I compare thee to a summer's day?
Thou art more lovely and more temperate…
Rough winds do shake the darling buds of May,
And summer's lease hath all too short a date."

She looked back at me and coughed with her mouth wide open. It wasn't a real cough, you could tell straight away that there was no phlegm in it or anything, and she only did the one of them so her throat can't have been that irritated. I moved back from her just in case it was something contagious.

"I wrote that poem just now for you while I was sitting here," I said.

"Oh," she replied. "What was it about?"

"Erm... hello? It's a love poem? *Shakespeare?*" I said, confidently. This didn't go down very well, and I decided to revert back to my original analogy. "Did you ever notice that the buses look like fish?" I continued. "Look. That one's a neon tetra. White body, pink and navy stripes." (You can check this information on the internet by the way, and you'll see I was right.) "That little yellow Anglian minibus with the blue markings – same colours as a damsel fish!" I said. "And as for that double decker that just passed? That's a purple tang. My dad bought me a fish tank, that's how I know all their names."

"Ah, here's my bus," she said, standing up and hurrying to the door, as if there were any danger of her missing it.

"This your bus is it? Black, yellow, red – those are koi carp colours!" I laughed in amazement at the fact that this was correct. It couldn't have gone any better! Or could it? What if I followed her onto the bus, carried on with my conversation? I decided to do it, and joined the queue, even though I had no idea where Halifax was. I made sure to stay one person behind her in the line because I didn't want to look like a stalker, plus, that meant I could choose where to sit in order to chat to her further. I thought about sitting in front of her. That way, I could sit like those Japanese yakuza do in films, with my legs spread wide apart and my arms rested on my knees, leaning forward with a "don't mess with me" attitude. I wasn't sure how well that would work unless I was smoking a cigarette or holding a weapon in true yakuza style, however, and with this in mind, I decided to pick up a Metro magazine on my way in and roll it up to make it look like a baseball bat.

The man in front of me asked for a single to Belstead Road, and I did the same when it was my turn to pay, instantly realising I ought to have bought a return ticket instead. It wasn't so much the money as the fact that a return ticket meant I wouldn't have to speak to the driver on the way back, and I was keen to minimise any contact with other men, in case they knocked my self-esteem. I leaned back in to the luggage area to let people walk past me so I could rectify my mistake, but the driver soon started up the engine and began to swerve out of the station. I staggered forward as the engine roared and shouted "Driver!" to get his attention, but he didn't hear me and continued on driving like a complete maniac. I could see from the corner of my eye that the girl I had recited poetry to was looking at me. Luckily, there was only one passenger on the seat behind her, so I decided to approach him.

"Hello there. I wonder if I could trouble you to move along a seat?" I said to him politely.

"No… you couldn't," he replied. He was a working class man wearing a rubbish coat but nevertheless I was

80

surprised that he refused to do me this favour - I could have easily been his boss's son for all he knew.

"I'm sorry, I don't think you understand my situation…" I smiled, despite the terror which was spreading through my chest. "My friend and I would very much like to continue the conversation we were having in the bus station…"

"Tough," he said. Now I'm no fool, and I quickly realised that if I were to continue trying to reason with this brute he would end up making me look foolish one way or another.

"Well, thank you for your time," I said. "I'm Alex Warren by the way. It was nice to meet you."

For some reason he laughed at this and replied "Oh yes! It was *charming* to meet you too, Mr Warren!"

I was rather pleased at this reaction – in the space of half a minute I had schooled this man in the art of polite conversation, and I felt a sudden rush of warmth for my little 'Eliza Doolittle', wishing I could sit down beside him and really give him my full attention – to heck with the girl!

The bus was thundering along at this stage, half machine, half beast, and it felt as though my eyes were being rattled out of their sockets as it roared along the road like some kind of hellish chariot. The din of the engine was frightening, and I wasn't comfortable at all with being forced to stand.

"Hello again!" I said cheerfully to the girl, who didn't look up. I tapped her on the shoulder to get her attention, but she flinched at my touch and shuffled away from me. How could I have been so stupid? I had chosen a shy girl on purpose, yet here I was, approaching her publicly. Of course, it would be better to get off the bus at the same stop she did and follow her down the road so that I could talk to her in private. I was about to sit down when the bus turned a corner very abruptly, and I realised I was in danger of having a serious accident if I wasn't careful.

I took a window seat at the front of the bus and tried to calm myself as best I could by focussing on my surroundings. Water lashed down on the windows and there was a comforting feel to the electric light, which seemed to glow all the brighter because it was a rainy day outside. The sound of the rain was terrific, and I would have been a happy chap if only I hadn't just made a fool of myself in public.

I was surprised at my fellow passenger's passive attitudes to the little romance that was developing in front of their eyes. When I had been talking to the girl, I half expected the little old man in the next seat to nudge her in the ribs and say "Go get him honey!" or something like that, but instead he had just glared at me as if I were some kind of sex pest. That kind of thing never happened to Adam Sandler, and I'm a lot less threatening than he was!

I kept craning my neck around to see her, but she was pretending not to notice me in that way girls do when they find you attractive. This put me at an immediate disadvantage, as it's well documented that prolonged eye contact releases the endorphins associated with love and speeds up the whole process of courtship considerably. Of course, I resented her a little for not knowing this, but at the end of the day that's what you get when you go for an ugly girl who is too inexperienced to understand courtship rituals because nobody has ever fancied her before.

The last time I turned around to look at her again, I was in for a shock, because she was chatting happily away to the man who had refused to move up and give me a seat. Not only that, but she was actually laughing! *No doubt he has just told her how much money he makes as a common chimney sweep*, I thought to myself. As amusing as it was to poke fun at the fellow, the girl herself was not without fault in my eyes. I'd gone to all that trouble to be near her and there she was, chatting away happily to my rival without the slightest shred of loyalty. This was not a woman I wanted to entrust with the responsibility of bearing my children – why I'd hardly even trust her to carry my shopping! Well – just like that, I fell out of love with her. In fact I soon became quite angry about her behaviour, and although I know some people would say that you have to love someone to get so angry with them, to me it was a clear cut case of never wanting to see her silly little face again.

This left me in quite an awkward position, as I was now headed out into the middle of nowhere on a rainy day for no reason whatsoever. I tried to determine our location. The windows were frosted with a fine layer of condensation which glimmered the colours of all the trees and houses we were speeding past, and I had no way of determining where we were. I was just about to press the red button for assistance when the bus pulled over, and who should get on but the most gorgeous young lady I had ever seen in all my life? Not only this, but she sat down next to me!

I realised at once that the whole day's events, from my offering my father a lift in the morning, to following him to the Marina, then wandering to the bus station, had been leading up to this encounter. She and I were destined to meet, it was an undeniable fact, and I knew exactly how to optimise my chances of getting it right this time.

Number one, I wouldn't say a word to her while I was on the bus. I'd learnt that lesson only too well! Number two, I would stare at her intently at every opportunity in order to make her fall in love with me. Number three, I would follow her off the bus.

Well, it wasn't long at all before I found my first clue about this girl, who I have completely failed to describe to you in my rush to get to the meat of the story. For a start, she had long, brightly dyed hair which was styled into 'dreadlocks'. It was a surprise to me that I found her attractive despite this - as you are already aware, I come from money, and as such I prize cleanliness very highly, but this girl was hourglass-shaped in a dumpy kind of way which actually worked, if that makes any sense at all? She had on these clunky boots that took away from the chubbiness of her calves most effectively, and to top it all off, she wore fishnet tights! She was obviously a true woman of the world – someone who would not flinch if you happened to brush her shoulder on a bus by accident, but laugh and carry on as if she thought nothing of it. My suspicions were soon to be confirmed - as we turned a bend, she leaned in to me a little, and I could feel her thigh pressing up against mine, which was absolutely thrilling.

I realise how grotty that sounds, but please believe that it was a genuinely erotic experience, and besides, it was *her* thigh rubbing up against *mine* – she could have manoeuvred herself away from me without difficulty. I took this as a sign that she liked me, and was content to sit there, taking in the details which would give me a conversational advantage. For instance, she had dog-hairs on her skirt, and the odour of tobacco on her coat was undeniable. Pets and cigarettes. I could live with them if I had to. Perhaps I could ask to 'cadge a fag' from her once we were off the bus. I would even let her light it for me, staring at her intently as she did so in order to release her endorphins.

I thought things through in this manner for some time, closing my eyes and savouring her musky aroma. I let myself imagine we were at home in the drawing room together. An innocent enough fantasy, straight out of 'Brief Encounter' - she with her knitting, myself with a crossword, the warm glow of the fire warming us as we savoured the music of Rachmaninov. It was a picture of domestic bliss!

When I opened my eyes she was inputting a text message into the keypad of her phone, and I sat there looking at her knee as the rain came down and the bus rumbled on. It was awfully romantic - every now and then I noticed a little hair poking out through a gap in her fishnets. It was the kind of intimate detail one doesn't notice whilst viewing women from a distance, and I wondered briefly if I should tell her about it. Perhaps not. I wasn't channelling *Dad* strongly enough, that was my problem. I spread my hand out on my knee in a physical display of strength. It was only a fraction of an inch away from hers, and I reckoned if she looked down she wouldn't be able to help noticing how long my fingers were, and marvelling at the alien nature of my masculinity.

By now the bus was trundling through the wilderness, but I had been enjoying the ride. The sight of the rain outside was doing me good and the air was rich with moisture. I think I'm allergic to summer – the heat, the insects and the bone dry air make me feel like I'm living in some dreadful post-apocalyptic society, with everyone trudging around the streets half-dressed. The weather that day had thus far been my friend, encouraging me out of my shell by providing the exact kind of environment I thrive in, and I had started to feel quite confident that today was going to be the day I sorted my life out.

I was just about to move my hand a little closer to this erstwhile un-worshipped goddess's thigh when her mobile phone started to make a dreadful racket. It was playing a song characteristic of the age, with the lead vocalist speaking, rather than singing, to a backing track of bongos, whoops and whistles. I remember being surprised that it wasn't rock music, as she looked like a 'goth' to me, and I thought to myself that this disparity between fantasy and reality would make a fine topic of conversation, but I needn't have worried about that, as her phone call was about to supply me with several.

"Ello?" said the girl, in exactly the kind of accent I hoped she wouldn't have. I have dropped the 'h' altogether in an attempt to recreate the way she spoke, but the truth is I've gone so long without being exposed to her vernacular that she might well have had her own curious way of pronouncing the letter which I am unable to express. She then went on to use all kinds of bizarre phrases which betrayed nothing at all about the topic of her conversation...

"Who says? No I ain't... No I never! Who says I done that then? I'll tell you what, when it comes to them kids right... when it come to them kids, there ain't nothink I won't do for them... Those is my kids and what they do ain't nobody else's business."

I had been reading a book about street gangs around that time and instantly realised that she had to be part of one. I liked the idea of being accepted into a group whose identity allowed members to remain 'other' in the eyes of society whilst still drawing support from other members. She had dyed her hair red and blue because these were her 'street colours' - I realised that now, and it intrigued me. Who had I got mixed up with? I put my hand back on my knee so she could see again how big it was.

I wondered how I would fare as part of a street gang. Thanks to the Virtual Reality Game Creation Forum, which I hosted online, my leadership abilities were sound - I had an IQ of 140 and excellent memory for names and faces, the combination of which might make me quite the Napoleon among my charges if I put my mind to it. By the way, when I say I have an IQ of 140, you can rest assured that this is indeed the case, and while I am aware that a majority of people lay claim to IQs of between 120 and 140 these days, most of these figures are reached far too hastily after a cursory analysis of their brainwaves. I did mine the old-fashioned way, participating in a complex multiple choice flash quiz online. I would have become a member of Mensa decades ago if it weren't for the fact I'd have to let them know where I lived.

As the girl yapped on about getting her 'benefits' and being given due 'respect' from her 'kids', I wondered what her position might be in this complicated social network. I assumed bed and board were included in the deal once one became a member, and I started to get excited despite the fact that deep down, I knew I hated everybody, friends and foes alike. As someone whose nerves were set on edge by the sound of a spoon scraping against a saucepan, I wouldn't be able to tolerate the antics that go on in gangs of that kind – waking up to find other people's socks on the floor, doing backflips in public or standing on the street at midnight smoking cigarettes in order to claw your way up to the top of the heap. Was it because I was falling in love with this girl that I was willing to contemplate such acts of madness for her sake, or was it the rhythm of the rain on the windows, lulling me into becoming someone else?

What if I were to follow this girl back to her base? For all I knew, her entire phone conversation was a ruse designed to attract potential recruits. After all, how would a street gang be able to recruit members who simply announced they wanted to join? Any number of undercover police might sign up only to turn around and arrest the lot of them on the spot. I imagine one goes through a similar process to join the CIA – a subtle series of hints and signs which one has to be finely attuned to in order to get through to the inner circle.

I was sure of it. This is what today had been for all along – not only had I fallen in love, but I was headed toward my new home, to take my place among men who'd accept me for the hard-hearted rebel I was. No longer would I have to apologise to Mother for the tiniest mistakes, like stacking my used dinner plates on the windowsill or leaving used tissues in my jeans pockets before putting them in the laundry basket. In a gang, if you so much as step on the foot of a fellow you outrank, it's they who must apologise to you! We had been travelling for a good fifteen minutes since the woman had boarded and sat down next to me – travelling into a new reality. I had stepped on the bus as a babe-in-arms, and I would emerge from it a man. Gone was the fearful loner who hastened to his room at the sound of his father's footsteps in the kitchen, and in his place, a warrior would stand.

When the girl finally pressed the bell, I started a little, and suddenly had an intense fear of getting off the bus. It was still raining outside, and I didn't have an umbrella. As I followed her onto the street I grabbed a Metro magazine, which it was necessary to hold over my head almost at once as the cold, hard drops of rain plummeted onto my bald spot, trickling down my scalp and leaving a filament of grit in my hair, which I was at such pains to get out that I almost forgot about the girl, who was marching ahead of me.

If only I had an umbrella! I thought to myself, for the second time in as many minutes, picturing the version of myself that did have one jogging along behind her, spreading the black parasol open and steadily offering her shelter. When she accepted, the *smart* me, the *prepared* me, the *me who always got it right*, held it over both of their heads, dipping to avoid a branch and edging even closer to her. I imagined the pair of them walking ahead - the *me who knew better* and the *girl I would never have*, running under a pine to escape the rain, leaning in to the shelter of each other, closer and closer. I would go about it carefully, kissing first her left cheek, then her chin, then her right cheek and finally her forehead, waiting until she was a trembling mess before brushing my lips against hers in a blissful first embrace. Only I *wouldn't*, because I didn't have a *damn umbrella.*

This irritated me immensely, not least because my mother had kept a veritable artillery of umbrellas in the ceramic plant pot next to the front door. There was one in particular, emblazoned with a bold hounds-tooth pattern which would have been perfect for the occasion of our first kiss. I tossed it to the imaginary me, wishing for all the world that I were him.

Now, the red haired girl was still on her mobile phone, and I was becoming so impatient with the way she lumbered club-footedly along in those impractical shoes of hers that I had to stop myself from overtaking her as she swerved slowly from one edge of the path to the other. Curiously enough, however, she seemed completely unaffected by the rain, and I found myself wondering if her imperviousness to it was a result of the kind of endurance training I imagine one has to undergo before joining a street gang.

There had been no sign of a house or village in sight for most of our journey, as we had been walking down a main road for some time, but suddenly a council estate came into view on the hill up ahead. It was a terrifying sight which only added to my already considerable misery. The rain was everywhere - hissing in the gutters, sizzling on the pavement, huge drops of it plastering my hair to my scalp, dripping from my nose and eyelashes, and the trees that grew alongside the road offered little protection from it. *If only her shoelace would come undone,* I thought to myself, *she would have to stop to tie it.* I couldn't think of any other reason she might have to stop, especially in this weather, apart from to cross the road, and so I decided to close the gap between us and catch her attention at the next available opportunity.

Finally, I saw my chance. She had stopped to take something out of her handbag, and dodging the various sprays of dark liquid that spurted up from the sides of the road as the cars whizzed by, I dashed toward her and yelled out, "Excuse me!" She didn't reply, speeding up her pace as though she was trying to get away from me, and in my desperation to attract her attention, I thrust my hand into my pocket and pulled out my wallet, yelling, "Excuse me, I think you may have left this on the bus!"

She stopped and looked at me.

"No, I never," she said. Then she frowned. "Which bus?"

"The one we just got off. I was sitting next to you."

"You followed me off that bus?"

"Yes, I thought you might have left this behind," I said, now very aware that I had offered her my wallet, which was positively stuffed with twenties. If I was going to give her money, she had to at least know it was mine so that she would feel obliged to 'make it up' to me when we got back home.

"Frr-eak," she said. The word rolled off her tongue in an animal way, part purr, and part growl. She took another look at the wallet. "Yeah, it's mine anyway," she said, holding out her hand.

"Erm, no it's not, actually," I replied, no longer in control of my faculties.

"Yeah, OK, whatever, ya fr-reak," she said, readying herself to cross the road. It was now that I realised I must either come clean or lose her forever.

"I'm so sorry, I think we've got off on the wrong foot. You see, I invented the ruse about the wallet as an excuse to start a conversation with you."

"Oh, get lost would you?"

"As it happens, I am rather lost, in fact I have no idea where I am!" I laughed, hoping to lighten the atmosphere.

"Good, now piss off," she said. Something in the way she said this made me feel as though there was little chance for us.

"What's your name?" I said. But she made no reply,

crossing over the road and continuing on. I marched alongside her on the opposite side of the road, shouting playfully over at her.

"Is it Mary?" I yelled. "Is it Samantha? Is it Rose?" She ignored me and started to speak on her mobile phone, which made me miserable, as it meant that her attention was fixed upon someone else. Finally, I crossed over the road and followed her, if only for the reason that I had nowhere else to go.

Soon enough I realised this was not the best option for either myself or the young lady, who was now standing in a layby on her own. I caught up with her quickly enough, feeling flustered at the sound of the traffic, which whizzed past us at ridiculous speeds. It was a jolly good job I'd decided to follow her after all, in case any strange men had taken it upon themselves to pull over to the side of the road and accost her that afternoon. "It's really pouring it down isn't it?" I said, staying on safe territory with talk of the weather.

"Look, what do you want?" she said, almost ugly with unhappiness.

There were so many replies I might make to her if I hadn't been so afraid of getting into a relationship with another human being. What *did* I want? Companionship? Yes. Love? Perhaps. Sex? Not necessarily – the opportunity to lay in her arms and drift into a blissful stupor would suffice. I had one last chance to impress her. I thought back to the romantic comedies I'd seen, and realised that this situation most resembled the scene in 'Four Weddings and a Funeral' where Charles (Hugh Grant) confesses his love to Carrie (Andie McDowall). This was partially because of the rain, but also due to the remarkable differences between our accents. Like Charles, I was a quintessential Englishman, but whilst his shirt got soaking wet in the confession scene, I was wearing a waterproof jacket, which gave me an added advantage as I would be able to concentrate on what I was saying.

I ran over the speech he made to Carrie in my mind, cutting out the references to marriage, which I was in no way prepared for, and editing it down into a manageable sentence. This process left me with the following phrase to work with: *'For the first time in my whole life I have realised that I only love one person, the person standing in front of me, in the rain.'* I didn't have much time to consider how to deliver this, so I just blurted it out, channelling the vulnerable Charles with all my heart and soul.

The laughter which followed was a knife to my heart, and she told me to go and 'something myself', if you can believe it! That 'something' was a word which I can't repeat here, or even hint at, but I am sure you know what it is she said, and to this day I can't get the vile image conjured up by her words out of my head. I was still reeling from the shock of this outrageous statement when a car pulled up, and out of it there emerged a very large and stupid looking man, who marched out of the car and took it upon himself to say much the same thing to me as Carrie had already, threatening me with actual body harm of a reproductive nature. It turned out to be the case that this great bearded Sasquatch of a man was Carrie's good friend, and from the look of him the gang leader to boot.

Suddenly it all made sense to me. I was being scouted to join their gang! Now was the time to prove myself, as it appeared he was engaging me in some kind of rap battle, during which the two parties traded insults until one man or the other won. I drew in a deep breath and thought very carefully about what to say next. For the sake of decency I will not repeat here what I said to that great, uncultured giant, but I made sure that my riposte was both risqué and violent in nature. In short, I told him what I would 'like to do to him' if I had 'my way' with him, and made sure he was in no doubt as to the intimate and unwelcome nature of my intentions. To be blunt I told I would 'X' him in the 'Y' with his own 'Z' if he didn't watch out. I delivered this insult in a comical way, laughing loudly afterward and pointing at him.

Without saying a word, he strode toward me, and I was so afraid he was going to try to punch me that I leapt out of the way, falling and twisting my ankle in the process. He shouted something vaguely inflammatory at me before heading back toward his vehicle, and soon they were speeding away down the road, no doubt having a good laugh at my expense. I lay on the grass verge for a good while after that, drifting betwixt this world and the next. "Carrie, Carrie, how could you do this to me?" I whispered to myself, wondering if she might come back to save me, but she didn't, and soon enough I realised that if I didn't pick myself up and get back to Ipswich city centre, I might die right here in the street.

Luckily I was only moments away from the bus stop, and because I'd crossed the road to follow Carrie, every bus that passed was bound for Ipswich. One trundled along before I even had time to decide whether or not I felt like crying. It started to hail just a moment before I got on the bus, a fact which the driver clearly wished to discuss, but I was too miserable to concern myself with small talk, swinging into my seat with the kind of devil-may-care attitude which can only come from having narrowly avoided a fight with Satan himself.

There was an old lady sitting in front of me. (I remember this, and every other detail from the day rather vividly, as it stood out so much from the rest of my life.) She took off her head scarf to fluff her hair up and I stared at what I saw there in fascination. It seemed to hover above her head like a sparse white cloud, beneath which the desolate expanse of her scalp stretched out like a bare desert. *How did she let that happen to herself?* I wondered. Surely she could dye it, or even have a hair transplant? It was a few thousand pounds, but what else was she going to use the money for at her age? That she should simply accept the degeneration of her crowning glory seemed impossible to me. To make matters worse, she was reading a woman's magazine advertising make-up, leather mini-skirts and finger nail polish, taking in each page slowly as though these were things she seriously intended to buy. I wondered why she didn't just go to bed and live out the rest of her life in quiet solitude, eating cakes and watching television. For that matter I wondered why *I* didn't.

It was then that I realised why – it was because I was wildly in love with Jodie, the girl at the doctor's reception, and couldn't live without her. Being unable to return to this modern-day ministering angel, I had been transferring my affections for her onto the shy girl and the abominable goth - I didn't know why I hadn't realised it sooner. I closed my eyes and tried to conjure her up, imagining we were sitting beneath a cherry blossom tree in the rain. There was a light shower in my fantasy, and tiny flecks of drizzle were falling onto her shoulders, lit by a silver beam of spring sunlight. A pale pink petal fell onto her shoulder, and as I reached out a hand to brush it off, she smiled at me. 'I wonder what it would feel like to kiss you,' I whispered to her, and there was a lazy gleam in her eyes as I leant forward to find out.

I longed to sleep - to fall into a world where she was real, touchable. I leant back in my seat and looked around me. There was something profoundly cosy about the bus. Perhaps it was the sound of the rain coming down outside, but I felt a sense of being at home, an awareness of someone I could be one day – of someone who could be with *me*. I leaned my head against the window and fell into a sleep so deep it verged on unconsciousness.

Now, I hate to sound like a broken record, but it was still raining when I woke up and got off the bus. I'd never seen rain like this before. It was raining so hard I'd heard all the metaphors for it already, passed from one commuter to another. It was raining cats and dogs, it was pouring it down, etc… I wasn't bothered about the rain at all due to Dad's Berghaus jacket, although the huge drops of water that kept landing on my scalp from the rooftops and the gutters were something of a nuisance, accentuating my thinning hair and darkening its ash blonde hue to a flat and lifeless brown.

This might not have been a problem if I hadn't already started to walk toward the doctor's surgery to see her, wet hair and all. After everything I'd suffered to be with Jodie, I had to make my feelings known. I tried to picture her face as I walked through the glistening wet street, rehearsing what I was going to say when I finally stepped up to the counter to declare my love. There was something about the fresh, silver gleam of the rain on everything that day that gave me courage. I felt young and reborn, and the things that usually bothered me didn't make a dent as I marched purposefully forward, happy enough to consider singing.

Finally, I got to the doctor's surgery, peering through its half opened blinds to catch a glimpse of her. I'd been racking my brain for the perfect romantic cinematic moment to match my sentiments toward her, and realised that this was 'Jerry Maguire' stuff, as it would involve me marching in to a place where she felt comfortable and blowing her world with a declaration of eternal love.

Now, I'm no Tom Cruise, but I've watched *all* his films, and as a result I know a thing or two about romance. For a start, I knew that a little bit of rain can go a long way in women-winning situations, and I was well aware of the fact that whilst the water dripping from my eyelashes was an annoyance to me, it made me look both sexy and sensitive to women, giving the appearance of sweat and tears whilst highlighting the youthful smoothness of my complexion. There's something about the animal sheen of rain on skin which never fails to make a man attractive. The scene I had decided to re-enact was the one where Tom Cruise marches into a room full of prattling, man-hating women and announces 'Hello? Hello? I'm looking for my wife.' What a line - but that's not all. 'OK,' he says as the lot of them stare at him aghast, their feminine nest despoiled by his unclean manliness, 'If this is where it has to happen, this is where it has to happen – but I'm not letting you get rid of me.'

Just like that, Tom lays it all on the line. Yes, in front of that tiresome pack of harpies, he bares his very soul in the name of love. I adore that scene. 'We live in a cynical world,' he says. 'A cynical world, and we work in a business of tough competitors. I love you. You complete me.'

I knew I would have to take out the line about tough competitors and play around with it a little, as at that stage of my life I had never even had a job, but I liked the challenge. I took a seat on the wall opposite the surgery to run through the scenario in my mind.

It was only once I'd been sitting down for a few minutes that I realised what a toll the day had taken on me. My back ached, my head pounded, my fingertips were numb and every now and again my whole body tensed up with agony and then relaxed again of its own accord. Wondering how Jodie would react, I got to thinking about Renée Zellweger's part in the whole scene.

I mean, nothing that Renée's character (Dorothy) says makes any sense. Her classic line, 'You had me at hello,' is a damn lie for a start. If you can somehow find a way to see this classic film, you'll notice that Jerry says 'hello' not once, but *two* times after walking in, and immediately afterwards the camera cuts to Dorothy's face, which is an absolute picture of disgust. I mean, she's looking at him like he's something she just scraped off her stiletto. Now if that's 'having' a woman, I've had more women than hot dinners, ha, ha, ha!

'You had me at hello...' Pull the other one, it's got bells on. By the way, whilst Jerry is humbling himself in front of her, Dorothy's friends are all acting like he's seriously stinking up the room. I mean, why did Dorothy put up with that? Gawping at the poor devil as he practically crawls around on his hands and knees begging for forgiveness in front of the most passive-aggressive bunch of misfits ever dreamt up by Hollywood? Every single one of those actresses was hand-picked by a leading Hollywood casting agent on the sole criterion of how utterly repulsed they were able to look when confronted by the sight of the world's most attractive man, and you mean to tell me that he 'had you at hello?' Nonsense. Who would subject a man they loved to such treatment in front of women like those? If he *had you at hello*, sweetheart, get rid of the lot of them and invite him in for a cup of tea and some biscuits!

No. He had to *beg* first, he had to humiliate himself in front of everyone, and that was exactly how I intended to win over this receptionist woman. I'd do it right in front of her patients, and to hell with the consequences! Sitting on the wall wasn't helping, however – I was having to stand up every ten minutes to stretch my aching limbs. You see, I couldn't go in to see her at once. I had to make sure I caught her round about the time the surgery closed, so we could go straight out for tea and cakes to cement our love immediately afterward. Unfortunately, this little plan had one fatal flaw, and that was the simple fact that I felt as though I were dying, because of the stress and the harsh weather conditions.

About an hour into my vigil, a sour pain shot through my ears which nothing could soothe. No doubt they were a fine shade of crimson, what with the rubbing, and the wind, and all of a sudden I realised that despite my father's Berghaus, the people who walked past me must think I was the worst sort of destitute. I might as well have been eating a cold Gregg's steak bake, I looked so poor and battered by life, but I continued on, humiliating myself, as she would have wanted.

Still, I'd had time to plan the scene down to the last detail. A fair few women had gone in to the surgery while I'd been sitting on the wall, and they would still be waiting to be seen by the GP when I flung open the door and strode toward her, my hair slick with rain, and announced that she'd 'had me at hello'. You see, I'd finally decided that *this* was the line the women actually loved – I mean nobody remembers what *Jerry Maguire* said in that scene. I had to watch the film five times to memorise it, but your average thirty-something woman back then only watched it twice, maybe three times in her entire life, and the line that got to them was always the one about hello. The other crucial part

99

of this plan was that Jodie would be obliged to say *hello* to me at some stage during the time we interacted with each other. It was part of the job to say 'hello' to a patient if one was a receptionist, after all. And so, I was able to plan the whole scene in advance - her surprise as I walked back into her life, a little dishevelled from the soul-searching I'd been doing, but a man who knew his mind - a man who was not letting her get rid of him this time.

Was it really so easy? I closed my eyes to visualise the scene – her standing there, taken off guard, my vulnerable yet masculine silhouette in the doorway, and the eyes of the patients upon me. A mixture of testosterone and adrenaline was surging through me, wreaking havoc with my chest. It was a pleasurable sensation, and I felt like running, singing, doing countless unpronounceable things. Instead I pulled down the zip of my Berghaus a little, ready for her to see me.

I couldn't be wrong about this - she would see me standing in the doorway, and know why I was there. What might come after that, I had no idea, but I was paralysed with delight at the thought that she might love me, and I was about to go in when who should stride out of the office but Jodie herself? She looked good. I mean, she looked *Hepburn* good.

"Hello! Hi!" I found myself yelling after her as she marched away from me, trying to think what my father would say. "Nice day for a cup of tea, isn't it?" I shouted, at the exact same moment that a terrible bolt of pain shot through my spine, causing me to cry out in pain.

"Excuse me?" she said. I had a feeling that she'd heard me just fine, as halfway through the sentence I'd emitted a loud yowl that must have measured a minimum of eighty-eight decibels, even when factoring in the adverse effects of wind interference upon the transmission of my voice. I rose to her conversational gambit, however, as it suggested she was challenging me in a flirtatious way, whether she realised this or not.

"I'm in love with you!" I yelled back. I got this line from a de-light-fully titillating episode of Buffy the Vampire Slayer, where Spike, the vampire with a soul, finally admits that he is infatuated with the immortally beautiful Buffy mid-fight. Of course, as ancestral enemies the pair thrash the living daylights out of each other afterwards, but every couple has its own dynamic, and where better to discover ours than in a big city on a rainy day?

"What did you just say?" she said, stopping dead in her tracks. I tried to read her expression for signs that she might try to slap me, hoping the blow would miss my ear, which was absolutely sour with pain at this stage and could tolerate no further aggravations, no matter how passionate their origins. I suddenly started to wonder just how good Spike had actually had it.

"I said, I'm in love with you," I said, looking right into her expressionless eyes and realising at that precise moment that it simply wasn't true. Yes, that's right – there was no use denying it. She was no different to anyone else, and my ear was killing me. "Now if you'll please excuse me," I said, unable to even look at her any longer. It was at this stage I hit rock bottom. I wasn't in love with her. I wasn't in love with anyone. I just wanted to go to bed and destroy an entire multipack of Wotsits in under three minutes.

I started to walk, and the more I thought about the day I'd had, the faster my stride became, until I found I was jogging. Soon, the jog became a run, and the run, as painful

101

as it was, seemed to open up some floodgate inside me –
some energy I never knew I contained, pulsing out of me
as the desire to scream until there was nothing left of me,
until every atom of who I was evaporated into rain. I didn't
want to love her. I didn't want to comb her hair, or
remember which colour toothbrush was hers, or learn the
name of her favourite childhood pet. I simply wanted to
disappear, and I couldn't make that happen. All I could do
was run – and run I did – from her face, from the rain,
from everything in the world but myself, the one idiot in
the world I couldn't escape.

Chapter Four

Of course, it would be great to pretend I ran all the way back to the train station, but I wasn't even out of her line of vision before I found myself doubled over at side of the road, watching the rain rush through the gutters. I staggered to the church railings, panting for breath like an asthmatic pensioner, and was starting to genuinely fear for my physical wellbeing by the time she reached me. For a moment I thought she might stop to help, genuinely touched by this rare display of male weakness. Maybe she'd find it so refreshing to have a man literally *run away* from her that she'd ask me out for a hot chocolate. These thoughts whirled into my mind as she approached, and dwindled just as quickly as she walked right on by, sniggering as she snuck a look at me. I was disgusted at her attitude, and decided to get even with her by going for a coffee with someone else instead, just to show her what she was missing out on. This decided, I stood up, smoothed down my coat and marched away from her as quickly as I could.

Now that I knew what I was doing, I tried to make a plan. As I mentioned before, my wallet was stuffed chock-full of money that day. You see, I never feel safe leaving the house without at least £100 in cash on me, in case there's a sudden apocalypse – I like to hand bank-notes to people in order to get away from them as quickly as possible. I mean, there's something about the sight of £20 that really shuts people up. If you're paying a cashier for an item, say a bag of potatoes, with a chip and pin card, the entire time it takes to enter your number into the machine, wait for the transaction to process, then collect your card and receipt back is loaded with a stupendous pressure to make small talk. It's all up for grabs when you pay by card – how you got here, why you bought such a large quantity of potatoes,

103

where you're going next or how busy the shop is. Cash, on the other hand, speaks for itself. Maybe it's something about seeing the Queen's face, challenging you to make small talk in the presence of royalty. You just don't. You maintain a silent respect. I think this applies just as much to smaller denominations of money as it does notes – there's something quite comforting about carrying all those tiny little portraits of Her Royal Majesty around with you, at least, to an English gentleman such as myself there is.

Anyway, I had plenty of 'dough', and I planned to spend it too. First I needed to go to where the women were. I sat on a bench outside the Post Office (the rain was a light drizzle by this time) and started to take notice of the ladies walking past, paying particular attention to the wildly varying assortment of shoes, coats, hats and skirts they were wearing. Mother always wore a blouse, a cardigan and a skirt made of rather stiff fabric, which only showed a glimpse of calf when you took the length of the socks she usually wore into account. These new fashions had certainly been lost on my mother, who knew how to dress for her figure, and never was swayed by the promises of 'A New You, Right Now' made by these magazines and television programmes. These ladies, on the other hand seemed rather susceptible to such promises. By all rights the lot of them ought to be dressed like Paddington Bear in this weather, but even the rain didn't seem to stop them from displaying inordinate amounts of leg and décolletage.

I made my way to the town centre, noticing that the storm had flushed the malingerers from the street corners. Gone were the slow-walking old men, the screaming toddlers with their insufferable mothers. This was a new world, with its gleaming wet streets and empty benches, and the only people to be seen were walking with such speed and purpose as to be almost tolerable, even to me.

This is one of the many things I have always liked about the rain. It stops one from dawdling on the unimportant, casting a sheen of purposefulness over everyone it touches. It brings people together too. All of a sudden I found myself able to look virtually any woman in the eye, gesture up at the clouds and find myself understood by them. There was only one more thing I needed in order to maximise my chances of success. An umbrella! But where could one be found? I went into a shoe shop.

"Got any umbrellas?" I asked the assistant who was standing at the door, looking out at the rain

"No," he said. There was something about this man's face that infuriated me. I know how judgemental this sounds, but the sight of him was incredibly aggravating.

"And do you have any idea where I might obtain one from?"

"Umbrella shop," he said. It was then I realised what was riling me about this individual. He was chewing gum… at work!

"Sorry, I'm not from these parts, whereabouts is that?" I asked, in order to ensure he gave me full instructions.

"Umbrella shop? Just up the high street mate…" He began. I listened to his answer intently. You see, if I had an umbrella, and a woman didn't, and I happened to be kind enough to share it with her… You see where I'm going? An icebreaker if ever there was one. Who could deny the respectability of a well-dressed English gentleman sharing an umbrella with a woman in distress? The assistant instructed me to turn left at such and such a road and head on past some statue or other. I thanked him for his advice, and was about to take my leave when he added,

"Nah, I'm joking mate, there ain't one. You just get 'em from the pound shop, don't ya? Ha, ha, ha!" I glared at him with disgust for a few moments, unable to believe what I was hearing.

"Do you wish to make something of this?" I asked him, ready to make good on my threat.

"You what?" he said, bursting into laughter. I realised then that he was too stupid to waste any more time on and walked in the direction he had indicated, wondering if he would ever realise just how close he had been to humiliation at my hands.

That was two fights I'd narrowly avoided in as many hours. Men obviously found me threatening - perhaps it was the testosterone flooding through my system after meeting so many potential mates in one day. I decided to limit all interactions with members of my own gender and stick to 'safe zones' such as department stores and florists until it was time to go home. Soon I was trudging from one shop to another with no idea of where I was headed. I looked in the windows of a few boutiques, amazed at the quality of the items on offer – I remember there was a pair of holographic sneakers, *for men, mind you*, that really caught my attention. At the time they seemed rather futuristic, and I imagined they would cost about £100. The surprise, nay excitement, I felt when I saw the price tag – (a mere £40) was thrilling. I mean, for that money I could have just taken them at home and enjoyed looking at them, but the assistant was a man, and my unfortunate encounter with the fellow at the other shoe-shop was enough to put me off the purchase.

I carried on walking until my attention was caught by a multi-coloured stack of soaps which lay out on display in a gaily decorated window. The sickly sweet smell coming from inside the shop was overpowering - I inherited an incredibly refined sense of smell from my dear mother, along with her rather large nose, and as a result I am unable to tolerate anything other than the most delicate of odours without recoiling instantly from the their sources. I was about to beat a hasty retreat from the place when an absolutely stunning young woman with bright pink hair stepped toward me and gave me the most marvellous smile imaginable. For a moment it crossed my mind that she might be a fellow gang-member of the young red haired lady from the bus, and when she greeted me, I had no idea how to reply. I needn't have worried, as she didn't wait for my response, telling me that if I needed help with anything I need only ask.

At this stage I felt the unfamiliar sting of tears behind my eyes, and had to tilt my head back a little to stop them from running down my cheeks right there and then. *If I needed any help I only had to ask?* It was as though she had peered into my soul and somehow figured out exactly what I most needed from a woman. I held my breath and walked inside.

Curiously enough, the shop seemed to sell soap almost exclusively. I tried to imagine how such a business would survive in my village, where general supplies such as white bread rolls are considered a scarce resource. What if you didn't *want* to buy soap? The shop space would have been put to much better use if the owners were to offer a wider variety of goods up for sale. I thought about suggesting this to the pink-haired girl as an ice-breaker, picking up a small, purple sliver of soap from the counter and taking a sniff of it. To my astonishment, the girl noticed me doing this and actually approached *me* to make conversation!

"Do you like it? It's a Blackberry Bubble Massage Bar. It has real blackberry seeds in it to exfoliate the skin."

She said this through a smile so wide it felt as though I might vanish inside it and be lost forever. She had hypnotised me - I mean *really* hypnotised me - if this fuchsia-haired siren had finished her sentence with a command to kill myself, I would have merrily obliged.

"Do you want to try it?" she asked.

I nodded my reply, grinning like a simpleton.

"Take a seat, I'll just be a second," she said, picking up a glass bowl from the counter and taking it into a room at the back of the shop. I watched her as she filled it up with hot water, realising that she was built like my mother, who wears a size 18, despite her modest B cup.

I had read my mother's Trinny and Susannah book about body shapes several times before I gained full, unsupervised access to the internet, and had always hoped my 'first' would be one of the lucky ladies in possession of a 'vase' shaped body, with slim legs, a gently curved waist and a large cup size. This said, I had also watched the Dove 'real beauty' advert several times, and knew deep down that you had to pretend not to care about these things in order to stand any chance with a woman. Perhaps once we were an item it would be possible to encourage her to put on a little bulk by taking her out for dinner every night of the week. It would certainly be worth the price of a few dozen portions of spaghetti carbonara to get her at fighting weight. By the time she returned with the bowl, now full to the brim with gently steaming water, I was prepared to accept her as she was for as long as it took to get her into a committed relationship.

What happened next is impossible to describe as delicately as I would like to, and I will leave it to the discretion of the reader to pinpoint the exact meaning of my words for themselves. Setting the bowl on the counter, she took my left hand in hers and rubbed the purple soap along my palm in a slow, sensual stroke that sent all the hairs on the back of my neck standing right up to attention. "Can you feel the seeds?" she asked me. *Could I feel the seeds?* I was physically unable to reply, every single muscle in my body stiffening up as she touched me. She dipped my hand into the water and stroked the white, creamy suds from my fingertips. "They're from 100% organic berries," she continued, conjuring up an image of all things ripe and fecund in my mind whilst I perched right on the very edge of my chair. She moved her finger a little, and I felt a tremor ripple up through my arm and across my back. I moved my shoulders to shake it off, but it didn't work, and when she smiled at me again, I felt as though my stomach was suspended on elastic threads, bouncing with pleasurable vibrations.

Finally, I could stand the torture no more, and I drew my hand away from hers, half euphoric, half mad, rubbing the aftershocks of her touch from my skin. There was no mistaking it - she was in love with me too. In fact, she risked her job by giving me such a sensual massage when she ought to be working. I had to stop myself from crying out loud with joy – there would be time for that later. Right now, I had to seize my chance to let her know I felt the same way.

I was about to say something when she picked up a tube of yellow goo and squeezed its contents into her palm.

"Now this one is a fully organic body treacle…" she began, rubbing the slippery liquid up my wrists with gentle strokes. I shifted in my seat, unable to decide what to do, and this sudden movement knocked the bowl, so that the liquid span around and lapped over the rim a little. She leaned over to wipe some spilt foam up from the table and as she moved I caught a whiff of her scent. It was intoxicating – like a childhood memory of strawberries and cream eaten on the brightest day of summer. Well, this was the straw that snapped the camel's back, and I realised I had to do something to distract myself before someone called the police.

I hastily searched my memory for a similar incident. The last time something like this had happened to me, Mother had been rubbing calamine lotion on my back, and in order to stave off disaster, I'd forced myself to imagine being made to walk the plank (a personal childhood fear of mine). Since then however, I'd come to find the thought of being captured by pirates strangely appealing, and so I tried to think of the most repugnant, irritating thing I had ever experienced instead.

I was left sitting in front of the television a lot as a child, and as such have many unpleasant memories of it. One of the most depressing things on TV back then was the advert for Birds Eye Potato Waffles, which used to make a regular appearance on our screens, due to the fact that the foodstuff itself was so unutterably vile that nobody would buy it unless the command to do so was inserted deeply into their subconscious. The advert was a garish, infuriating hodgepodge of vibrantly ugly foods set to an intolerable, jingle-jangle backing track, which was being sung by a man who sounded as though he were being simultaneously strangled and drowned at once, and just the thought of it made me absolutely furious.

"Do you remember that bloody awful advert for Birds Eye Potato Waffles?" I asked the assistant in desperation.

"Erm…" she said.

"Birds Eye Potato Waffles, they're waffley versatile!" I sang, springing up from my seat like a jack-in-a-box just in the nick of time. Needless to say, my life might have been a lot different if that damn advert had never existed. I imagine we'd be married with children by now. If there's one thing I've learnt from that miserable episode, it's never disguise your true feelings from a woman, no matter how embarrassing they might be at the time.

"Oh-kay…" she said, in that way women do when they mean that they hate you and wish you were dead. I realised it was now or never.

"Would you like to go out on a date with me?" I asked, fully expecting her to say no.

"Erm… no?" she said. Her reply seemed to take the form of a question, which gave me the impression she might have conflicting feelings.

"Why not?" I asked. "Didn't you like my song?"

"Not really, no."

"Shall I compare thee to a summer's day?" I began.

"No thanks," she said.

"Oh… alright, then." I said, trying to stand. "Do you mind if I ask why, or…?"

She appeared not to hear this question, walking over to the doorway to welcome in another customer.

"Oh wow, it's really pouring it down out there, isn't it?" she said, in a voice so insincere that it sent chills up and down my spine. There had been no hint of this in her voice when she spoke to *me* whatsoever, and to this day I can't quite put my finger on the reason her feelings toward me altered so suddenly whilst mine had remained so rigidly unchanged.

I waited until she was looking the other way and dodged out of the door before she saw me. The moment I stepped outside there was a flash of lightning in the sky, and I have to say I liked this tremendously – it made me feel as though I was the star of my very own 'music video'.

I took a look around the high street and breathed the wet, concrete scent of the city deeply. People were standing in doorways to avoid the rain, cowering under their outspread coats and running through puddles left right and centre. It was as if an enormous bomb had gone off, and as I walked through the street, allowing the sensual little rivulets of rain to bathe my skin, I felt the eyes of those who were taking shelter roam upon me freely. Silvery water rushed down the gutters at either side of the street, sparkling on the road and simmering in black circles that filled my shoes as I walked through them.

It was a simple enough trick, succumbing to the soft, wet freshness of it all - I simply imagined I had stepped into a cool shower after a long, hot day of playing videogames in my fleece jumper, letting myself relish the feel of water on my skin. Oh, the water was everywhere. Everywhere! Spurting in torrents from the rooftops and flaring out from the roadsides as the buses soared past. I delighted in the attention I was drawing from the women who watched from their various places of safety as I was gently pummelled into submission by its little wet fists, and by the time I reached the traffic lights I felt like some kind of weather god walking among my subjects, striding through the vibrant currents of water that splashed out at all angles from passing cars.

What a day, oh what a day! I was wet to the bone, and up ahead the thunder was growling away in the dark grey sky. The excitement of it all had made me hungry – hungry for life itself, and as it just so happened, the shop across the road was a KFC. Now Mother never allowed us to eat there, and whilst I'd smuggled a box of chicken nuggets into the house in my school bag after a school trip once, the 'Big Mac' was still a delectable mystery to me. One which I now meant to decipher, bite after forbidden bite. I was so excited at the prospect, I almost got run over, and by the time I'd dashed into the restaurant, my heart was pounding away as if it were Christmas morn.

The restaurant was almost full, and there were two customers ahead of me, which gave me plenty of time to try and make out the different kinds of food on offer. There was a wonderful smell in the air, and if I hadn't been soaked through I believe I would have wanted to stay there forever, just soaking in the warm and lively atmosphere.

The woman in front of me completed her order and stood to the side, waiting for it to arrive. Ironically, in my rush to give my father his glasses, I had left my own in the car, and I took his out of my pocket and tried them on for size to get a better look at the gaily illuminated menu. I was trying to figure out whether or not they improved my vision when the little assistant addressed me in an unhappy voice.

113

"Yes, one Big Mac hamburger please," I said.

"Yeah, we don't do those, sorry." Now I 'don't speak woman', but something about the way she said this indicated that she thought I was an idiot and I felt as though I had to show her I had a lot of money in order to make up for this.

"OK, what's the most expensive thing on the menu?" I asked, leaning over the counter with my wallet out so she knew I meant business.

"The deluxe boneless feast," she said.

"Certainly, I'll take two of those," I replied with a curt smile, taking two twenty pound notes from my wallet and folding them with a single hand. I had learnt this trick from father personally one evening when he was particularly drunk and needless to say, the teacher had soon become the student, as I was well practiced in the art of card tricks back then.

"What drinks would you like with those?"

"Please, won't you decide?" I replied, with a courteous bow.

"We've got Pepsi, Diet Pepsi…" she began, but I wasn't listening. Instead, I gazed down at her skinny fingers, looked up at her mournful brown eyes. How I wished our circumstances could have been different. If we were on a date, I would let her choose my order for me and then share it with her right down the line - the poor girl certainly deserved that kindness.

"You decide all that for me, please," I said. She mumbled something shyly without so much as a glance back up, and listening to the racket her co-workers were making, I wondered if anyone among them had the slightest idea that a mortal angel was working in their midst. I, for one, intended to acknowledge that fact to the best of my ability.

"Shall I compare thee to a summer's day?" I began.

"Any dips? Sauces?" she said.

"Oh… yes, please."

"Mayonnaise? Sweet chilli?"

"Yes, yes, whatever you think… Shall I compare…"

"Can you stand to the side and wait for your order, please?"

I was starting to wonder if Shakespeare had really had as much luck with women as his plays lead us to believe. Of course, even if he had been terribly unlucky in love, I suppose he would have never reflected this fact in his plays. I mean, just imagine if Juliet had been telling Romeo that a rose by any other name would smell as sweet, only to be asked in a shrill voice to speak up, or keep off the grass – the whole thing would have ended very badly indeed! As for Shakespeare himself, the fellow must have recited this sonnet to a number of women over his lifetime, and where had it got him in the end? One thing was for sure, it was getting me nowhere.

Instead of persisting with the sonnet, I tried to think of a scene in a romantic comedy upon which to base my parting shot to her, but before I had the chance, a huge, angry looking gent with tattoos shouted out my order number. I

115

stepped forward, showed him my receipt and lowered my head in a gesture of submissiveness. He seemed to understand this instantly, placing a heaped tray of food in front of me and grunting something at me. There was far too much food for one person to eat and he had clearly given me the wrong order, I knew that at once, but had no idea how to go about telling him.

"Excuse me," I began, but he had already yelled "Next!" in a brash voice, and as I had seemed to come out very much on top of the deal, I made the decision to accept his judgement and steal away with the banquet he had seen fit to place before me.

Despite my desperation to speak to the cashier again, I chose the furthest table away from the order point, as I didn't like the look of the fellow with the tattoos and suspected he had noticed that I was in love with his colleague. He looked like the kind of brute who could intimidate a girl into 'being his woman' before she'd even had the chance to so much as take tea with him, and no doubt he'd set his sights on her long before I came onto the scene. If he should wish start a fight over her, I knew I should face him at my full strength, and so I decided to eat my fill before making a move.

Finally it was time to turn my attention toward the food. There were a multitude of greasy paper containers and dips in front of me, and I chose a box at random and pulled out a crispy morsel of chicken. Now this was not the kind of chicken I am accustomed to eating, I want to make that clear. Until that very moment, if you had asked me what chicken tasted like I would have replied with some innocent nonsense like 'Sunday afternoons' or 'Mother's love'. This was something else entirely, and the moment my hesitant teeth cracked open that deliciously moreish batter and sank into the tender white meat, I became a ravenous, unstoppable monster, thrusting my fists into the box of chicken and cramming big flat handfuls of the stuff into my mouth.

Quite frankly, it felt as though I were 'having my way' with someone whom I loved very deeply, and with unsurpassed joy, I tore a battered chicken fillet in half and watched the steam escape from its secret depths before devouring both halves at once. Next, I tore open miniature packets of seasoning and shook them with vigour over the golden fries before seizing a dozen with each hand, letting their salt-bright surfaces christen my fingers with their delicious grease. Mind awash with images of youth and eternal life, I tore open the plastic wrapper that covered the butter-wet corn and sank my teeth into the firm yet yielding rows of it, relishing the sensation as they popped and seeped sweet liquid onto my tongue.

The Pepsi was lukewarm and frothy in my mouth, with bubbles so dense that it took half a bottle of it to quench my thirst - and yes, *I drank it straight from the bottle*, locked in the embrace of a rapture that only feast after famine can bring. I had spent my whole life in famine - being thrown scraps of attention at carefully timed intervals by a family who only kept me alive out of pity. But not today. I opened another little box and inhaled the savoury steam with tears in my eyes, tipping out palm-full after palm-full and feasting on them until I was a sensuous mess.

I tried to open the dips I'd been given, but my fingers were so wet with the various juices the feast had produced that I was forced to tear the lids off with my teeth, and I plunged the jagged white edges of the torn chicken strips into each sauce in turn, savouring the tartness of the sweet chilli dip, relishing the comforting tang of mustard, and the

117

letting rich smoky odour of the barbeque sauce drift cross my palette. I ate the fourth bag of fries in a couple of mouthfuls, and all the while, as I chewed and savoured the tender meat, I felt like a god.

I felt I could do anything – run miles in the rain, kiss a stranger or swear at a policeman, and face no consequences for my actions. Little wonder people become so addicted to these fast foods, I thought to myself, noticing that my hands were shaking. It certainly had an enlivening effect upon both my body and soul, and the more I ate, the more certain I became that the girl at the till, that frail, bashful little cherry blossom among a thousand lesser flowers, would be receptive to my advances.

My initial hunger pangs satiated, I poured myself some more Pepsi and gazed at her from the rim of the paper cup, watching her toil over the counter. She was serving one customer after another with an expression of pure exhaustion on her face, and I was suddenly reminded of the ending of 'An Officer and a Gentleman,' with Richard Gere and Debra Winger. Here I was, with my money and my father's car, sitting around and having a fine old time whilst she was slaving away in the daytime and more than likely living on the streets at night. Here was a girl who had to be rescued, and I was the very man to do it.

The end of 'An Officer and a Gentleman' has something of a bad reputation among certain feminists. 'What if she *likes* her job?' they cry. 'Cavemen behave better!' Still, they continue to swoon at the sight of men who dress up as Richard Gere at parties. My mind was made up. I would do precisely what *he* did – walk over, pick her up and carry her away into the sunset. There were a few details out of place of course - I didn't have a motorbike outside, for example, and my clothing left something to be desired in

118

comparison to his full naval regalia, but the Berghaus jacket was smart-looking, and certainly not to be looked down upon by an employee of KFC.

I rehearsed the scene in my mind. After finishing my meal, I would stride confidently toward her. It would be tough getting behind the counter without being apprehended by the tattooed rogue who'd served me earlier, so I took him out of the equation for the time being, sure I could find some way to distract him when the time came.

Now, Richard Gere has perfected the art of the confident stride – he never comes across as being too cocky when he does it due to that puppy-dog look he puts on his face, and with this in mind, I decided I would try to smile for this occasion, which is something I find very difficult. I tried to think of a happy memory to put me in the mood, and was immediately reminded of a wonderful week I'd spent locked in my bedroom playing 'Guild Wars' after swapping bedrooms with George. I'd stopped eating altogether by that stage and Mum had been so concerned for my wellbeing that she made me a hot turkey and stuffing sandwich on a real teacake with lashings of butter scraped all over it. She'd done this at precisely the right time, as I'd been so miserable wandering through the burning ruins of the city of Ascalon with my level 20 wizard that I'd just deleted the character and started the game again as a novice Ranger. This was a terrible decision game-wise, as it takes a long time to get to level 20, but the first level of the game was set in a glorious pre-war utopia, with rolling emerald hills, fields full of flowers and leafy green trees which swayed ever so gently of their own accord. This was in the days before there was very little difference between virtual reality and real life, of course, and it's difficult to describe how happily one could be transported into another world in those days simply by gazing at a flat, pixelated image, but it was possible, believe me, especially if it were the only means one had of roaming around the countryside freely without being shouted at by one's mother.

The ranger I created had free-flowing hair and a panther as a companion, and the relief I felt at watching her stroll happily about the forests, shooting the occasional bear and picking up gold coins was immense. I had just reached level two, and was standing by a pond watching the clouds drift by, when Mother knocked on the door with the sandwich for me. I'd devoured it more or less on the spot, grateful tears running down my cheeks, as I knew how much Mother hated to handle meat of any kind. I washed it down with a huge china mugful of Twinings tea, basking in the sun which streamed in through the closed blinds, and I remember thinking that my life wasn't so bad after all. I wasn't starving in a third world country – I wasn't being forced to work in some grotty little shop, or being hassled by an angry wife. I was just bored, that was all.

I closed my eyes and imagined the soothing music of the videogame, hoping just a little of that happiness would wash over me for long enough to allow me to maintain a warm, convincing smile as I walked toward her. Then, I would dash behind the counter and lift her from her spot at the till whilst her jealous workmates looked on disapprovingly. Whispering something reassuring in her ear, (perhaps even telling her if she changed her mind once we got outside I'd put her down and never bother her again), I would pick her up and give her a chaste, tongue-less kiss. After that, I'd probably have to pop her on the counter and collect her from the other side for practicality's sake, carrying her at an angle just sharp enough to ensure her hat fell off like Debra Winger's. Then, as her hair tumbled around her shoulders, I'd carry her out of the establishment to the sound of rapturous applause. Not for *her* the drudgery of menial work! She could keep my mother company, water the plants in the back garden, *anything* but dish out chicken to strange men who were utterly incapable of appreciating her unique beauty.

Of course, there were a few details it would be impossible to recreate for her, apart from the uniform and the motorbike. It wouldn't be quite the same without the classic song 'Love Lifts us Up', and I couldn't very well rescue her from her life of drudgery with a carrier bag of chicken slung over my arm. The thought of this was incentive enough to get stuck in, despite the fact that most of it was cold. I laboured on for ten minutes in this manner, focussing on the corn cobs, which Mother would have insisted I eat first if she were there because they were so full of fibre.

It was getting dark outside. The clouds had a faint pink tinge on their undersides, and a patch of blue-grey sky was peering out from behind the rainclouds. Suddenly a thought hit me – what if something went wrong? Even if it didn't, even if my plan *was* successful, I would be carrying her to the train station in the pouring rain, and the weight of the girl would add a good ten minutes to the journey. What would we talk about on the way to the station? What if she became conscious of her 'hat hair'? It was very wet outside, and she would be wearing no coat, so we'd only have the Berghaus between us. Slowly but surely, as I ate the cold, limp fries and picked the batter from the popcorn chicken, the plan began to unravel. It was no good. I took a last look at her, with 'Love Lifts Us Up' still playing in my head, then put the remnants of the boneless feast into the paper bag that the tattooed man had provided, and walked out into the rain without looking back.

Chapter Five

The chintzy little shops were beginning to close their doors now, sales assistants with mops and buckets glaring out at us from their clean, dry sanctuaries. I wasn't interested in their wares one bit. In fact, my main concern was that the paper bag that held my chicken was becoming dreadfully wet. Luckily for me, as I continued to make my way to the station, I happened to pass a branch of Poundland! I strode in merrily, making a great show of wiping my feet in order to reassure the security guard that I wasn't one of those mouth-breathing idiots who'd been treading wet debris over his nice clean floor all day.

Oh, what delights I found there! The place was luminous with products of all sizes and colours – I can't even begin to describe the kinds of things they sold - toys for cats, toy cats for children and even toy children for adults, all stacked up in gaudy arrays. I gazed at them as I walked past, half fascinated, half aghast, unable to understand how a shop like this, which actually sold objects made of *metal* as well as plastic, could do so for only one pound per item, regardless of the original value.

Why had I never been here before? There were several items which appealed to me as I wandered around, and I was seriously considering spending money on a pump-action container of liquid soap that had been expertly put together by some genius to look like it had a fish living inside it when I happened to pass the DVD section. Delighted at what I saw, I scrutinised the films with an attentive eye. Many of them were of little interest to me – old men talking about trains, children's TV programmes and documentaries about the war, and I was about to leave when I noticed that one of the DVD covers featured a rather beautiful woman wearing a pink two piece outfit. It was a copy of 'The Beautician and the Beast', a reasonably good film featuring the magnificent Timothy Dalton as an East European dictator who mistakenly hires a make-up artist (Fran Drescher, a voluptuously lovely leading lady) as his child's teacher. I won't add include any spoilers here, but needless to say I was delighted at the opportunity to buy it for the price of a mere pound coin and dropped it into my basket gleefully.

It had been right there on the bottom row, placed so that none but the most discerning of film buffs would even cast it a second glance, and when I looked along the rest of the shelf I discovered a glut of romantic comedies, both classic and obscure, which were so rare as to have had covers made up for them especially so that they could be sold here. Up for grabs were multiple copies of 'All About Steve', 'Good Luck Chuck', 'Kissin' Cousins', 'The Love Guru' and 'Man Trouble', all wrapped in cellophane to be sold to the drooling masses at a price so insulting that it actually infuriated me that there were any left on the shelves.

"Don't you people have any taste?" I muttered, picking out one of each film. My hands moved swiftly, creating two neat stacks of DVDs in my basket so as to leave room for the umbrella. Chief among the celluloid jewels was 'Fool's Gold', the invigorating tale of an estranged treasure hunting couple (Kate Hudson and Matthew McConaughy) who discover that the riches they seek are nothing compared to the discovery that they still love each other. I was very happy about finding this film here, as the few times I'd caught it on television I'd wished I had the DVD so I could 'visit' more often. The whole film is set on a shimmering Mediterranean isle with golden sands and an aquamarine sea, and is a delight from beginning to end. They scuba dive, water ski, lay on the sand and exchange several passionate kisses over the duration of the film - it's like going on honeymoon from the comfort of your sofa.

Delighted, I took two copies of the film, in case one should break, and it was this realisation that set me into a panic that they were being sold as defective copies. Indeed, the more I think about this, the more it made sense, as several of these films could easily still have commanded the £12.99 or so an average DVD cost back in those days. It was at that moment that a plump woman in a bright red coat tapped me on the shoulder.

"I see you're a film buff, a bit like myself!" she said. I frowned at this hodgepodge of a sentence, then continued to squint at the films, hoping she would take the hint and leave me alone.

"I love these old romantic comedies, me," she continued. *Me, me, me!* The woman was absolutely self-obsessed! Her hair was a woolly mess and she had a gap between her front teeth wide enough to wedge a pencil eraser into. No wonder she loved those films so much – she was hardly a leading lady herself and it was instantly clear to me that she lived her love life vicariously through these films. I almost pitied her, but not enough to relinquish my grasp on a single DVD in my possession. She reached over and picked up a copy of 'The Proposal', her wet red coat making a maddening whooshing sound because of the cheapness of the waterproof fabric. I hadn't noticed 'The Proposal' before, and I became convinced it was the last copy.

"That's a terrible film, you know," I told her, hoping she would put it back.

"Oh I don't mind, I just play them in the background to keep myself company," she said, tucking it under her armpit and picking up another one I'd been looking at. The title wasn't familiar to me, but it had a picture of Freddie Prinze Jr on the front and looked terrific. Never in my life, before or since, have I hated another human being as intensely as I hated her at that moment. I was about to tell her it only had a one star rating on IMDB when an unpleasant sales assistant came toward us.

"If you could just make your way to the tills please, we're getting ready to close now," she said.

"Certainly, madam," I said, in my debonair way, looking at the pair of them with an annoyed expression on my face so they would feel unwelcome and leave me to it, but neither woman had the common decency to comply.

"Yes, yes, I just have a few more purchases to make," I said, looking through the DVDs as quickly as I could and grabbing anything that looked remotely romantic. Luckily, I recognised the covers of some of the more iconic ones at a glance, and noticed that The Woman In The Red Coat was making as if to put the Freddie Prinze Jr film back on the shelf. I stared at the film unashamedly, hoping she would get the message and relinquish it, but instead she kept on looking up at me. It was most uncomfortable, and unable to bear the tension any longer, I made my way to the till.

There was a man in front of me buying all kinds of dried instant snacks the likes of which I had never seen before. They were almost like fish-food, dried flakes of starch with a savoury coating. And they wonder why the lower classes have such a high death rate? Vegan food preserves one's innards well into the nineties, and I have little doubt that the poor fellow must have died decades since, despite having been ten years younger than me at the time we were in the store together.

The Woman In The Red Coat was still looking at me, and in order to distract myself, I took to counting the DVDs in my basket, noting with annoyance that I only had nineteen of them, which meant if I handed the cashier a twenty pound note I would have to wait for my change. I couldn't stand the thought of this, and decided I would rather leave without the pound, but of course I knew that would cause a furore, so I grabbed a box of chocolates from the display in front of me to make it up to a round £20. When I did this I noticed that The Woman In The Red Coat was still gazing at me, and I cast a few glances back at her, if only to see whether she still had the films I wanted in her hand.

"I like your coat," she said. "It's a lovely colour. I might get one of those myself, mine's a bit worn out."

"Ha!" I replied. "Do you have any idea how much this coat cost?"

"No, how much?"

"A hundred and seventy pounds," I replied triumphantly. "Still thinking of buying one?"

"Oh no, no, I couldn't afford that," she said. "Oh well, guess I'll just keep on wearing this old thing!" Strangely, this answer did not satisfy me, and I was about to carry on explaining the features of the coat to her when she spoke again.

"That's a lot of movies you've got there," she said, smiling. "Do you live alone or something?" The impertinence of the question was absolutely astonishing, and to add insult to injury, she had used the word 'movie' to describe a film completely un-ironically. I shook my head in disgust at this. "Oh, do you live with your girlfriend then?" she asked.

"I'm sorry, is it your custom to ask personal questions of strangers or have you made an exception in my case?" I asked her plainly. "If so, please don't do so again, I find your line of questioning most impolite." She didn't have time to answer, however, as it was my turn at the till, and I certainly didn't mean to turn around and address her a second time.

The woman at the till was handling the DVDs very roughly and I listened carefully for the sound of a loose disc rattling in its case, deciding to sue if one of them were damaged.

"Pouring it down out there isn't it?" said The Woman In The Red Coat, more loudly than was necessary. "Trust me to choose today to leave my washing out! My cat's somewhere out there too, roaming the streets!"

The cashier had finished manhandling my DVDs and was busy jamming the box of chocolates into the carrier bag. When she'd finished this little performance I thrust the £20 at her, desperate to leave the premises before The Woman In The Red Coat started telling me what time she liked to get up in the mornings or how much she liked tea.

"Are you a cat person or a dog person?" she enquired of me boldly.

"Madam! I believe I've made it plain that I no longer wish to speak to you, now kindly leave me in peace!" I exclaimed. What business was it of hers whether I preferred dogs or cats after all?

"But why?" she said.

Ignoring her, I took the bag of DVDs and got out of there as quickly as I could, worried that she would pursue me through the street asking inane questions about favoured brands of detergents and so forth. Her lack of self-awareness was astonishing to me, as she seemed to labour under the illusion that I might have the slightest interest in a word she said. The shops were almost all closed now, and the vivid peach glow of the streetlights lit up the blue-grey sky beautifully. I realised I had forgotten to buy the umbrella, and that it was too late to even attempt to go back to the pound shop – no doubt someone would have something to say about it if I did – where was I going? Didn't I know the shop was about to close? Why did I still live with my parents? Yadda, yadda, yadda.

Funny, but now that I was well away from The Woman In The Red Coat, I felt myself begin to miss her a little. I know this sounds strange to say, given how irritated I had been at her impertinence, but looking back at the episode now I can honestly say that I somewhat enjoyed its cosy domesticity. Of course, back then, walking through the rain and laden down with bags, I didn't realise this, and only felt the loss of her company subtly. For instance, whenever I looked down at the DVDs, I was reminded of her, and all of a sudden there seemed to be an awful lot of people wearing bright red coats.

The station was only a minute's walk away at this stage, and god knows I needed to get home, but a curious sadness was flooding through me, and as the cars crawled past, their silvery lights illuminating the rain, I turned back and began to head toward Poundland again. I was walking against the crowd now, as people headed out of town back to their homes, partners and pets. The Woman In The Red Coat had wanted to know if I was a cat person or a dog person, and more than anything in the world, I suddenly wanted to tell her, but not there, in the dark at the edge of the road. I wanted to tell her by a crackling fire, over hot chocolate, on a starlit evening, in our own home.

I searched for her face in the crowd, thinking it ought to be easy to pick out her tasteless red coat and Poundland bag from among the dull colours of the well-dressed professionals. It wasn't, of course, and soon enough, the flow of human traffic heading toward me started to make me panic. The never-ending torrents of rain had contorted the faces of the travellers, whose glistening skins and gaping expressions gave them an unsettling alien appearance. I stood there for a few minutes hoping she would walk past, before realising it was hopeless and joining the crowd that flowed toward the station, a sea of people gleaming darkly beneath the newly lit streetlamps. On my way in to the station, I passed an old man who was busily sweeping water from one part of the room to another, and I marvelled at the futility of his work. He looked a lot like my father, and I wondered if Dad might have fared any better in a pointless job like this one.

The tungsten light of the station snapped me out of my confused stupor, and gazing up at the wildly fluctuating arrival and departure boards, I realised I had to ask for help or live out the rest of my days here, like Tom Hanks in 'The Terminal'. I contemplated this scenario for a moment, comparing it to my circumstances back home – the fellow ended up with lots of friends, free food, minimal living expenses and one hell of a kiss from Miss Catherine Zeta Jones – a lady who found him endearing for the sole reason that he was living rough in an airport. The lifestyle Tom had championed in this film certainly appealed to me, but I doubted things would work in my favour if I were to emulate the situation myself.

Perhaps the most unbelievable thing about that film was Ms Zeta Jones's interest in Tom Hanks. Tom has a habit of signing up for roles in which he is the centre of attention in my opinion. Take 'Castaway', for instance – it's all me, me, me with Tom in that film. Lots of people think the character of 'Wilson', a discarded basketball who becomes Tom's best friend in the absence of human company, is meant to be a futile symbol of man's need to connect with man. Unfortunately, the truth is a little uglier. Tom hates to share a stage, simple as. I, for one, would have found 'The Terminal' far more compelling if Ms Zeta Jones's character was stranded at the airport instead. I would have been fascinated to see how she washed, dressed and used her feminine charms in order to extract favours from passers-by, but of course, she would have kicked Tom to the curb if he'd tried it on. He wouldn't be 'special' enough for her if he was just a normal person.

Then there's 'Forrest Gump'. Now, in my opinion the only reason it took so long for Forrest and Jenny to get back together in that film was so that the magnificent Robin Wright (Jenny) couldn't steal the limelight from Tom while he was gallivanting around being all things to all people. I mean, they made up this whole plot where she turned from a happy, well-adjusted love interest into a shameless hussy, 'spending time' with other men, partaking in drugs and other illegal activities, simply so that they could halve her screen time with Mr Hanks. Give me a good Drew Barrymore/Adam Sandler pairing-off any day of the week over his one-man vaudeville acts. Now *there's* a couple who know how to share the limelight.

I glanced back at the old man who was sweeping the water out of the door. He looked exhausted, and the sight of him combined with all that brooding on 'The Terminal' had put me off the idea of starting life afresh in the station, so I joined the queue for the information booth instead, where a man was making a rather impolite enquiry.

"Who says I can't use ticket on that train?" he yelled at the poor bespectacled wretch behind the counter, water flying off his coat as he spoke. "Have you any idea how much money this ticket cost?" Whilst he continued to spit and gesticulate in one of the most infantile tantrums I have ever had the misfortune to witness, I stood behind him calmly, as if unaffected by chaos taking place all around me. It is the ability to disguise the continual rage that simmers beneath our calm facade which separates us from the animals, after all. It was a hellish place, though, and the longer I waited, the more annoyed I became at the businessman, whose voice had been gently rising in pitch and timbre the entire time I had been standing behind him.

I glanced up at the arrivals and departures board again – it might as well have been written in hieroglyphics for all the sense it made to me, and as the little monster of a man continued on in his rant, I realised that if I were asked to describe hell to a small child, I would paint him an accurate picture of my own circumstances at that very moment. I was soaked through for starters – my socks were wet, and the shoelace of my left Adidas trainer had tucked itself under the arch of my foot, where it nestled like a corpulent worm. My jeans sagged wetly at the knees, and their hems were drenched with mud. In fact mud was everywhere, streaked across the floors, splashed all over the backs of people's coats and pooled around the doors at the station's entrance, despite the old man's best efforts. It seemed to be a rule in this cold, soulless enclosure that someone always had to be screaming or running around in a panic in order for the place to operate effectively, and the unintelligible tannoy announcements were just as confusing as the babbling of the commuters, whose trains were being cancelled left right and centre because of the weather.

None of this seemed to worry the idiot in front of me, however, and he had just pulled up the waistband of his trousers, no doubt readying himself for another rant, when I felt a surge of adrenaline rise up inside me. There's only so much aggravation a man can take before he is compelled to act, after all, and I determined to make my mark upon this halfwit's memory with a cutting remark or two of my own.

"Pardon me," I said to the man, tapping him on the shoulder as he spoke.

"Shut it, stupid!" he replied. His quickness to make assumptions about my Intelligence Quota cut me to the quick, but I continued on, confident I was a 140, and determined to be heard by him.

"I wonder if you would mind calming down and continuing on with your enquiry in a peaceful manner?" I said, casting a tentative glance at the woman in the information booth, who was rather beautiful beneath those glasses of hers. "I'm sure the lady is willing to assist you in any way she can, after all."

"Shut it, you tramp!" he shouted in a downright confrontational manner. I hadn't been expecting this, and was about to raise the alarm when a large fellow in British Rail uniform appeared beside the woman in the booth and called out, "Next please."

Relieved, I went to him, avoiding eye contact with the miserable wretch beside me, who had quietened down considerably since the appearance of this modern day Hercules who, incidentally, was clearly in love with his female co-worker. I told him where I wanted to go and asked the quickest route to get there, watching his large, golden hand move as he wrote. It hovered close to the woman's arm, and I wondered if he had ever tried to force his affections upon her during the time they'd worked together. Perhaps they'd already given the relationship a go and decided it could never work. I hoped that this was the case, and the moment the disgruntled customer had gone, I caught her eye. "I'm sorry you had to deal with him, my dear - what a frightfully difficult individual he was!" I said, giving her a gallant half-bow.

"I'm not your dear," she replied bluntly before gesturing to the next customer.

"Excuse me?" I replied, finally pushed to my limit. "That man just stood there and verbally abused you for five minutes and got off scot free! What makes me the villain of the piece?"

"Platform 9," the man said, "Five minutes. And no more trouble from you please, sir."

"No more trouble from me? I called her my *dear*, is that a crime?"

"I've warned you sir, now make your way to your train before I have you removed from the station," he said, standing in front of the woman in a caveman-like gesture of ownership. Miserable and humiliated, I turned my back on the scene, and drifted toward the gates in an unhappy trance. I was astonished to find that my eyes had become warm with tears. I blinked them back. Why did everybody hate me so?

I thought again about Tom Hanks – how every character he ever portrayed on screen was an utterly clueless, average Joe who was loved by every woman he met despite his best efforts to repulse them with his obvious inadequacies. This made him the exact opposite of me – an intelligent, exceptional man, despised by all females within a thousand mile radius despite his best efforts to win their affections with his innumerable talents. It's almost as though Tom Hanks was somehow once supernaturally aware of my existence and made these unbearable films in order to taunt me from beyond the grave. The man was my natural born enemy, the lion to my gazelle. Thanks to 'actors' like him, outstanding men such as myself, who have dedicated their lives to furthering their education are shunned by brainwashed consumers of romantic fiction who won't look at a man twice unless he's just got his shoelace stuck in an escalator and has no idea how to get it out until he's fallen into someone, preferably a vulnerable young woman.

Falling over themselves! One after another, women fall over themselves to get a slice of Tom's perfectly unremarkable little life. In 'Joe Versus the Volcano', for example, Patricia (Meg Ryan) falls in love with him not *despite* the fact that he has depression and wants to kill himself, (something I would personally find very reassuring) but *because* of it, going so far as to follow him into the volcano after he literally decides to *commit suicide* rather than marry her, like the wet-nosed loser he is. Naturally, the volcano erupts and ejects them into a happy ending, brainwashing yet another generation of women into believing that things always work out for the best when you fall in love with hapless losers. Frankly, I would have appreciated a more realistic ending, with the pair of them vanishing into the lava forever, although it would be tragic due to the loss of the excellent Meg Ryan, an actress of such magnificence that literally every second of her life captured on celluloid, including outtakes, interviews and blurred paparazzi shots of her eating burgers, has made the world a richer place in which to live.

Unfortunately, she was one of the only actresses Tom Hanks was willing to share a stage with (no doubt he fancied his chances with her in real life) and I have endured many bittersweet cinematic moments because of this. Take the final scene in 'You've Got Mail', where Kathleen (Ryan) and Joe (Hanks) meet as themselves for the first time after concealing their true identities as online lovers. This is one of the only kissing scenes between the pair of them I can watch without having to physically obscure Tom's face with a cushion, due to the ingenious technique which the director used to film the two of them together, showing first Joe, then Kathleen, then Joe, then Kathleen, walking toward each other to the strains of 'Somewhere Over the Rainbow' in a way which makes it look as if they are each standing in two separate films right until the moment they meet.

The final kiss is a stroke of genius, as it only focuses on one actor's face at a time, filming Tom over Meg's shoulder, then Meg over Tom's, which makes it entirely possible for one to imagine that Meg is kissing Jeff Goldblum, for example, or that Tom is smooching Ellen DeGeneres, neither of which is as conflicting a sight as the two of them sucking face together. During the wide shot of the kiss itself, which risks showing both of them clearly at once, the pair press their faces together so closely that neither of their facial features are recognisable at all, and I can only imagine that the director was well aware of the unpalatability of the pair, and constructed the scene in this way in order to minimise the time they were seen touching each other on screen. Personally, I believe to this day that body doubles were used for the entire love scene, but no doubt Tom's team have covered the whole thing up. After all, who wouldn't want to kiss Tom Hanks? Me, for one, and Meg Ryan wasn't too keen either, mark my words.

My train was due, and I didn't know what to do about it – the seemingly endless tide of people was making me nervous, and after glancing at the board in a panic I went over to the old man, who was still sweeping up water by the doorway.

"Excuse me, friend, I'm rather new to the art of train travel and am trying to get to Diss station, could you please tell me the best way to go about it?"

"Platform 9," he said.

"Thank you kindly. Please accept this money as a token of my appreciation," I replied digging around in my pocket for a twenty pence piece to give him and dropping it into his palm.

"What's that for, then?" the old man said.

"Oh, it's for your trouble," I said.

"You can keep it," he replied, throwing it back at me as though it were cursed. What a strange man! I couldn't understand why someone like him would turn down money, unless he was some kind of holy man who was paying penance for his sins by engaging in unpaid menial labour. But still! Even monks must buy robes and crucifixes! Perplexed, I left him to his work and ran to the ticket barrier. It was only when faced with the prospect of actually going through the barrier that I realised I still had no idea where Platform 9 actually was. I rummaged around in my jeans pocket for my ticket, and as I thrust my hand deep into the denim folds, one of the paper handles tore off my bag of chicken. I was still able to hold the bag by scrunching it up at the top, but I felt as though this made me look like a 'wino', and became afraid that people might mistake me for one of the street sweeper's friends if I went back to ask him whereabouts Platform 9 actually was.

Unable to cope with the sheer volume of problems I was facing, I wandered over to a man in uniform and explained my situation to him at length, fighting back the tears. I think at some point I mentioned how angry Mother would be at me if I didn't return home, and that after I said that he realised he had better let me in for her sake, and opened up the disabled barriers to let me in. Hurrah for the good old fashioned English gent! I hoped never to encounter another street sweeper in all my living days. In most films worth watching, street sweepers are a different breed entirely. They hand out sage advice to the protagonist while leaning on their brooms, lay out the law of the land to bedraggled travellers, or give valuable advice on the travails to come. This fellow had nothing to offer me whatsoever but a catty remark over a trifling sum of money, and hadn't shown the slightest interest in assisting me through my plight. If I hadn't been in such a rush for the train I would have gladly reported him to his superiors.

By the time I reached Platform 9, the train had 'pulled in', and there were fifty or so people waiting for it to empty. Foremost on my mind at this stage was the fact that, with my Poundland shopping, wet clothes and crumpled paper bag, I would be refused entry onto the train for breaking the dress code, and so I walked calmly towards the first carriage I could see, and was about to get onto it when I noticed something astonishing. It was The Woman In The Red Coat, stepping on to the next carriage. I was about to run to her when the platform assistant shouted at me to get onto the train, and I obeyed immediately, grateful that he would even consider allowing me to board in my dishevelled state.

Chapter Six

Almost as soon as I had stepped onto the train, the doors began to close, and I realised that I had chosen the worst carriage imaginable. I was standing by the toilet in the vestibule, surrounded by an array of misfits in all shapes and sizes. There was a dirty, chemical smell in the air, and as the train set off, I steadied myself by putting my hand onto the wash-room door, almost falling through it in the process. This embarrassed me greatly, and in a panic, I let myself in, closing the door behind me so that everyone watching got the impression that I had meant to do it.

Well, once inside I actually started to brighten up a little. It was rather a squalid little wash room, but it had a futuristic feel to it which, combined with the unfamiliar hum of the engine and the sound of the rain on the windows, gave me the feeling that I was travelling through space in some kind of miniature escape capsule. Better yet, this was a nice little private place for me to gather my thoughts and figure out a plan.

The first thing to do was to create some more room in my Poundland bag so that I could fit the chicken in it, and I had a good idea of how to do it too. The whole time I'd been walking back to the station, the box of chocolates I'd bought had been poking out of the bag, sticking into my calf and causing me no end of grief. It was one of those little annoyances that one can only bear for so long before tearing something valuable to shreds in frustration. With this in mind, I decided to eat them and throw the box away. The idea of putting cardboard directly into the bin instead of recycling it without Mother finding out was rather thrilling, and I made a mental note never to confess this to her for as long as I should live, no matter how long after the fact it might seem. The toilet seat was down already, and so I sat on it and set my Poundland bag on the floor, keeping the chicken balanced on my knee so as not to contaminate it with the germs from the toilet. I took out the box of chocolates and tore it open, popping one into my cheek and letting the sweetness settle on my tongue. Well - what a sensation! I couldn't wait for the chocolate to melt, and when I bit down there was a crisp, sugary shell which released an incredibly delicious liqueur-flavoured centre. My hands moved automatically then, scooping another three out of the box and cramming them into my mouth. How could something so cheap taste so good? I scoffed the last of them as the carriage rocked from side to side, and was folding the box flat so I could cram it in the tiny bin by the toilet when I caught a glimpse of the ingredients list. They had contained not just flavouring, but *actual brandy!*

At first I thought I had to be wrong, but when a sudden light-headedness hit me, I knew it could not be otherwise. In a blind panic I staggered to the sink and turned on the cold tap, meaning to drink from it until the effects of the alcohol were neutralised, but the thought of the innumerable germs that clung to the tap's spout was too much for me, and I sat back down on the toilet to try to compose myself.

Without thinking, I started to eat the cold chicken in the hopes that it would soak up some of the alcohol, but the combination of the food, the booze and the constant movement of the train made me feel queasy. Further adding to my physical discomfort was a general sense of anxiety over the fact that by now, my fellow passengers must all have assumed I had some kind of terrible stomach complaint. Right then and there, I made a vow to myself never to leave the house again, wishing with all my heart I was back at home watching YouTube clips in bed with a nice big mug of tea and some digestive biscuits. *This* was not, after all, how a gentleman spent his evenings!

How remote the possibility of such a peaceful retreat seemed, as I sped through the darkness in an illuminated tin tube full of strangers who couldn't care less if I lived or died. The alcohol was beginning to take effect by now, and I realised that if I didn't get out of there soon I was likely to pass out whilst still locked in there. Steeling myself for the humiliation of emerging from a toilet I'd occupied for some fifteen minutes, I pressed the unlock button and strode out as confidently as I could, winding a path around the bystanders to the next carriage in order to save myself the indignity of looking the ones 'who knew' in the eye.

Funnily enough, I'd somehow managed to forget all about The Woman In The Red Coat during all this kerfuffle, and I was genuinely surprised to see her standing at the end of the carriage. As soon as I saw her I knew I was going to do something stupid. Maybe it was because I was drunk, or maybe it was love – I'm not sure why, but I knew that if I didn't go over there and knock her socks off, I'd regret it for the rest of my life. The people all around were little more than extras on a cheap film set to me now, gawping at tablets or chatting to each other in that self-satisfied way 'normal' people do. They didn't fool me! I used to spend whole nights reading their feelings on internet confession sites – mothers who hated their children, husbands having affairs, the list was endless. For all its sunsets and long summer rains, the world was an ugly place. It had to be, because if it wasn't, I had wasted thirty years of my life hiding away from it! I couldn't stand the thought of that, and suddenly couldn't wait to get back home to Mother.

If it hadn't been for The Woman In The Red Coat I would have kept my eyes closed until we reached my station, trying to blank out the misery all around me. The thing was, *she* had loved those films as much as I had. Those films, which were the closest thing to a perfect world that anyone could wish to see. She had spent her life walking silently through this babbling crowd of liars, cheats and simpletons, heading toward the same glistening shore I had stood upon alone all my life, waiting for her. And all I had to do was walk towards her.

The rain was something else by this stage, streaking the windows as we hurtled through the darkness, and the sound of the train both lulled and excited me simultaneously. I walked down the aisle and sat on a seat which gave me a good enough view of The Woman in the Red Coat so that I could leap up if it seemed she was about to leave and follow her off the train. I sat there for ten minutes, avoiding making eye contact whenever she noticed I was looking at her and hoping the smell of my chicken wasn't disturbing anybody. A few times I was tempted to look through my DVDs, but I was half afraid The Woman In The Red Coat would come over and ask if she could borrow them.

I decided to approach her with a totally straight face. It's been proven by a hundred different weekly magazines that men who don't smile are deemed more attractive by women. In 'Atonement', for instance, Robbie (James McAvoy), rarely smiles at Keira Knightley's Cecilia. During the fountain scene, when Kiera dives into a fountain in a see-through dress, he glares at her as she emerges from the water, frowning as though he were gazing in the direction of the sun. Women love this stuff. Brad Pitt does it in 'Meet Joe Black'. Plenty of blinking and lip biting going on as he gazes into her eyes, oh yes, but not a smile in sight. I've seen this technique used time and time again. Just a slight frown and a gentle tremor of the lips is enough to hook a woman for good. As the train began to slow down for Diss, I decided to give it a try.

Still sitting down, I stared at her intensely to catch her attention, and the instant she looked at me I scratched my nose and looked away assertively. The booze had really started to kick in now, so much so that I almost laughed out loud when the moron next to me answered his phone by saying "Y-ello" instead of 'Hello'. Mother did a fine job of teaching me how to speak correctly, and I've never had much time for individuals who chop and change the letters of perfectly good words in order to carve themselves out a 'regional identity'. There are two English accents as far as I'm concerned. 1) Correct English, *meaning* as close to RP as possible, and 2) Mispronounced English. That everyone else fails to grasp this simple fact, carving letters from words as if they were cancerous tumours, is a source of continual amazement to me.

I stared at The Woman In The Red Coat's reflection as she gazed out at the neon blue sky beyond the window. Her mirror image glowed in the glass like a translucent mask of unhappiness, and a few times it seemed to stare straight back at me. At the time, I was thinking of the scene in 'Twilight', where Edward Cullen first meets Bella Swann. As he's staring at her from across the refectory he has this intense look of misery (verging on pure hatred) on his face. Of course, this is because he wants to drink her blood, but as far as she's concerned it's an attractive expression - you can tell she likes it from the way she bites her lip. I was saving that technique for when I was up close and personal with her, so I didn't lacerate my delicate mucous membrane tissue.

It wasn't long before the voice on the tannoy announced that the next station stop would be Diss. I stood up immediately, stepping on my paper bag at the same time as I lifted it, which caused it to tear right in half. This was a minor disaster, as no sooner had the paper torn away than the bottle of Pepsi rolled under the seat, the French fries spilling out all over the place. Whether people laughed or not I couldn't tell you - I was too horrified to notice. I could just about bring myself to write off the chips, but I was unwilling to give up on the chicken, stacking the boxes on top of each other.

I picked up the Pepsi and crammed it into the bag of DVDs, making my way to where the middle aged woman stood. If she hadn't noticed me before, she did now. Everyone did, because the food smelt so delicious. I did a full-on Edward Cullen, staring at her with a dark and troubled expression and not once taking my eyes from hers. To my delight, she looked back at me, and as I approached her I bit my lip, dipping my head slightly before slowly letting my eyes meet hers. The train had stopped now, and the time was ripe to act. I lunged toward her and began to speak.

"Shall I compare thee to a summer's day?" I said, realising how drunk I sounded at once. A half smile fluttered on her lips, however, giving me a clear sign to continue on. I had started to sweat and my voice was tremulous with nerves. I tried to pretend she wasn't there, that I was at home reciting it in the bath, this poem I'd said aloud a thousand times over, to the mirror, to the treetops, to the women on TV and in magazines, and now to her – as if it was the last thing I would ever do that had any meaning.

"Shall I compare thee to a summer's day?
Thou art more lovely and more temperate.
Rough winds do shake the darling buds of May,
And summer's lease hath all too short a date.

144

Sometime too hot the eye of heaven shines,
And often is his gold complexion dimmed;
And every fair from fair sometime declines,
By chance, or nature's changing course, untrimmed;

But thy eternal summer shall not fade,
Nor lose possession of that fair thou ow'st,
Nor shall death brag thou wand'rest in his shade,
When in eternal lines to Time thou grow'st.

So long as men can breathe, or eyes can see,
So long lives this, and this gives life to thee."

My heart beat fast and I felt faint, but I had said it. People were starting to board the train now, and in a few moments I would have to step off. I was close to tears. It hadn't been enough, I knew that. She wasn't going to follow me off the train, or give me her phone number or confess her love. I had said the poem, and that was that. What kind of a man was I? I couldn't create a tribute like that to her in a million years. All I could do was stand there like a fool and recite it, hoping this would somehow change my life. Then, she smiled. I liked it so much that I held out the carrier bag full of DVDs and thrust it into her trembling hands.

The last person had stepped onto the train, and I stepped off it and onto the platform, my heart racing. The door closed a moment later, and I turned to see her smiling out at me and saying something with one hand pressed against the glass, like Cecilia on the bus in 'Atonement' when she's leaving Robbie behind, and like Robbie, I broke into a run and followed the train as it set off, drunkenly shouting "I love you!" But she couldn't hear me. I watched the train until it was a dot in the distance.

145

The rain bounced off the tracks, settling in pools among the rubble below, and people were looking at me, but I didn't care. I was a hero, I was one of the good guys. I was in love.

Chapter Seven

I instantly regretted giving her the DVDs, however. I hadn't even had a chance to look at them, and had been sure there were a few rare gems in the bundle that would have sold for three times the amount I paid for them if I'd had the sense to list them on Ebay. The money in my wallet represented a whole year and a half's worth of birthday and Christmas money combined, and my parents made sure only to pay me on those two occasions. I had even had an inkling of an idea that I might set up a small shop on Ebay which specialised in rom-coms. That was all gone now, and so was she. I had never even found out her name.

Still, I had the remainder of my boneless chicken feast to look forward to. It was my intention to freeze the rest of it once I got home, and with the loss of the DVDs it suddenly became imperative that no further disaster should deprive me of the remainder of it. The platform was quite clear now, apart from a single female station guard, and I realised that it was better to get my keys out here in the light than risk my personal safety locating them by the side of the car. I was glad of the distraction of the lost keys, as in the back of my mind, I had been thinking about The Woman in the Red Coat and wondering if I would ever see her again, which was a feeling I didn't enjoy at all as it made me feel all fluttery inside.

Finally, I realised it was pointless looking for something with one hand when two could be used, and I stacked the boxes of chicken up on the bench beside me so I could open up the jacket and look in one of its many inner pockets. The networks of zips and press studs were a little confusing, but after patting myself down I located a small hard bulge under my left rib which, I hoped, could only be the keys.

Can you imagine a disaster more perfect than the zip breaking as I pulled it down? Well, mid-zip, I felt it stick. In my rush to put the coat on as I followed Dad into the station that morning, I'd zipped my t-shirt right up in there. Of course, it took me a while to realise this, but after a few moments of gently tugging at it while the panicked strain in my bosom slowly rose to a crescendo, I panicked, and yanked the zip so hard that the slider snapped off it completely.

This was a major disaster. I tried to re-attach the slider to the zip, but there was no figuring out how to do it, and to make things worse I'd nicked my finger in the process, which made any further fiddling about with it rather painful. Going home with it broken was not an option - I couldn't even begin to imagine the arguments that would take place because of it, but go home I must, before the storm caused a major obstruction on the road. The station guard walked past me now, readying her whistle, and I realised that here was a woman who wore a coat *every single day*. She would surely know what to do!

"Excuse me, but the zipper of my jacket appears to be broken," I said to her. "Do you know how I might be able to fix it? I have a long walk home in the rain and might catch my death of cold."

"Let me see," she said, walking over and looking down at the jacket. She was wearing a smart suit and had a matronly manner about her which I found rather attractive. A train passed by on the opposite line with a comfortable rattle and hum, and the hiss of the rain on the shelter above was doubly soothing in her presence.

"Do you have the original zipper?" she asked. I held it out

to her, and as she examined it I was reminded of the scene in Brief Encounter where Alec (Trevor Howard) helps get to get the grit out of Laura's eye after a train passes by, but my heart wasn't in it, and all I could hope was that she would fix my zip or die trying.

"No, sorry, I think it's broken," she said, walking down the platform toward the train that was pulling in. Realising I had time to take get out of the way of the crowd before they got off the train, I piled the boxes of chicken against my chest and walked to the car park, startled by how quickly my exposed t-shirt soaked up the rain. Father's car was easy to find, and I piled the boxes on the bonnet whilst locating the keys, which were indeed zipped up in the inner pocket. It was then that I noticed a piece of paper stuck to the windscreen wiper. I tore this in half and let it fly on the wind. Apparently this was a parking ticket, but I couldn't have cared less at the time. I put the puller of the zip in my back pocket, no longer trusting the coat to do its job, and opened the car door, piling the chicken into the passenger seat and slamming the door closed behind me.

As I started up the engine, a dark huddle of people made their way out of the illuminated entrance. They looked like alien invaders stepping out of a spaceship, and as they wandered toward their cars, I turned on my windscreen wipers, obliterating them one after another. Suddenly I had the desperate urge to drive away as far and as fast as I could. Perhaps I could live in a bus shelter for a while – there was a cosy-looking one made out of stone in a village just along the way. I could sit there like some kind of local eccentric, just watching the world go by. I swallowed hard, the faint aftertaste of the liqueur still lingering on my tongue. Only a drunk could dream up plans like these, I thought to myself, following the blurred red tail-lights of the car in front and driving slowly through the blue and gold-tinged city.

The rain's metallic crackle on the car bonnet had intensified by the time I reached the main road, and jets of water rebounded against the windscreen like great showers of sparks. I thought about The Woman In The Red Coat, still whizzing through the dark landscape on board that distant train, and wondered if she were thinking of me too. It was possible, and I felt a glow of excitement at the prospect. I slowed the car down to a crawl, following the signs for home, which were barely visible through the storm.

The road was a grey blur before me, sparkling lines of rain illuminated in the headlights, and it was falling down so hard it sounded like everything in the world were being torn apart at once. I was on a lone country road now, following the shining painted lines and little red lights that were studded along the side of it. It felt like some magnificent disaster was about to happen – first, a fox darted through the grey-white ray of my headlights, lit up like a phantom, then, as the cars drifted by like shooting stars noiselessly traversing the dark, a neon flash of lightning electrified the black night sky. As I drove on into the storm, barely conscious of the danger I was in, I realised that this had been the best day of my life by a long distance.

The sound of a police siren snapped me out of my reverie, and I glanced in my mirror to see it was speeding toward me. I found a safe place to stop at the side of the road so that it could pass, and as the vivid red and blue lights glimmered into the distance I realised how lucky I had been not to get pulled over and breathalysed. An awareness of how drunk I was hit me all over again - I'd made some pretty silly decisions since eating those chocolates, spilling junk food all over a public vehicle, giving away £19 worth of goods to a perfect stranger, making a public declaration of love and breaking the zip of my father's coat clean off. I was feeling sleepy too, and while the rain was bouncing off the windscreen in a fantastic display, I was having trouble keeping my eyes open.

There was nothing for it – I couldn't risk the drive home. I made sure the road was clear and pulled out just as another flash of lightning lit up the horizon. Suddenly terrified, I determined to drive to the nearest village, park the car safely and hire myself a taxi home. Onward I drove, through the fantastical landscapes of the countryside at night, hypnotised by the lights that glowed, shimmered and burst forth from the water in explosions of electric colour. A lone motorcyclist sailed by like a ghost, and I watched them disappear into the horizon with a wistful sigh. If the rider was a man, he was going home, to sit by a fire or make love to his wife. If she was a woman, she was going to need to shake her hair out of her helmet, get out of those wet clothes and stand by the fire as soon as she got home. Either way, I wanted to follow that bike to the cosy glow of whichever country cottage its rider was bound for.

But I couldn't - I was stuck with myself forever, compelled by genetics and instinct alike to spend the rest of my life hidden in the wilderness, with my family. I was thirty four already, and time was running out. It was only now, as the lightning flashed a third time and the rain obscured my vision that I started to become truly afraid, and when the illuminated island of the nearest village loomed toward me it was all I could do to find a reasonably safe space to park and stagger into the murky little phone box by the side of the road.

There were several business cards for taxis stuck up in the

booth, and I phoned the first one I set eyes upon, instructing the fellow at the other end of the phone of my whereabouts and returning to the car to collect my fried chicken, which I realised would spoil if I were to leave it in the car overnight. After a few more minutes in the rain, the boxes had become so wet that they sagged in the middle, and in a moment of drunken inspiration I took off Dad's Berghaus and covered them with it, letting the rain run down my bare neck in a slow and sensual embrace. There were no passers-by at all but the occasional car, and when the taxi driver arrived I made it plain to him that I'd had my fill of conversation for the day.

I gave him directions to my house, sat in the back seat and rested my head on the window as we sped into the fray. Somewhere out there, The Woman In The Red Coat was almost home. *Somewhere out there.* That was the name of the song in 'An American Tale'. I sobbed quietly as I remembered the scene where the two little cartoon mice who have been separated sing the same song from different parts of the city whilst glancing up at the moon. I opened my eyes and stared at it myself, with the words of the song running over and over in my head.

"Somewhere out there
Beneath the pale moonlight
Someone's thinking of me
And loving me tonight."

I cosied down in my seat, remembering the beautiful smile she had given me. It was finally true. Someone loved me - someone was thinking of me. I closed my eyes and snuggled under the Berghaus, clutching the chicken. Wet and cold as I was, it was warm in my heart, and the whole world felt like my friend as I fell asleep to the sound of those tiny mice singing.

I woke up just as we neared the approach to my driveway, unbuckling my seatbelt and thanking the driver in advance for the ride in order to make sure he realised how desperate I was not to have a conversation with him. He seemed to understand, and in my haste to leave, I agreed to his unreasonable demand for the £60 fare without as much as a murmur of protest. After a day wandering the streets alone in the rain, the cottage ought to have glowed like a beacon of hope in an unforgiving world toward which one gravitated uncontrollably. I felt nothing but dread at the sight of it, however, and only wanted to spend a few more minutes outside, looking up at the stars. The face peering out of the drawing room curtains had other ideas. It was George's. The game was up.

I hadn't planned this far ahead, stepping out of the taxi and balancing the chicken against my chest as I closed the door. The coat was still draped over it, and I wouldn't be able to put it on unless I set the whole meal down on the front step. I had determined to do just this when my mother strode out of the front door, screaming.

"What the hell is going on, Alex? George is beside himself! What are you doing? What's that you've got there?" she yelled as I walked in, balancing the chicken and the coat against my torso. "You're soaking wet! Where's your father? That's his new coat! Oh my god, you've *ruined* his coat!"

Suddenly I could see why Dad had shot out of the door at first light every morning despite having lost his job. It was this house – he couldn't stand to be in it any longer. How hadn't I see it before? Until now I had thought my parents co-habited in this unfinished mess of a house in much the same way Tom Hanks and Shelley Long had tolerated each other in 'The Money Pit' as Mr and Mrs Fielding, a highly-strung, wealthy couple who struggle through all kinds of misfortunes in the pursuit of their ideal home. Where they had fought in public over the repair of a window or the replacement of a tile, I imagined my parents had made up in private, laughing over how angry they had been at each other only moments ago. Suddenly on the receiving end of my mother's accusing stare for the first time in my life (I had never defied her in this manner before) I realised that we would not be laughing about this incident in the morning over coffee and croissants. No. Instead, it would stand between us like an unseen stone, pressing against our most sensitive spots every time we came close to one another. Mr and Mrs Fielding didn't have time for such things, because they only ever spent one hour and fifty one minutes in each other's company.

I had lived in this house with my family for thirty four years, and in all that time never once noticed how extraordinarily ugly it was – how everything inside it decayed over time, how stiflingly small its nooks and crannies were compared to the limitless expanses of land outside, how quaint its inhabitants – those niggling, petty little individuals, constantly finding fault with each other, people who had opinions on everything and were always right, no matter how farcical their ideas.

"Give me a moment," I said to her as I closed the door, suddenly feeling rather ill. For the first time in my life I was struck by the utter grottiness of the house – its stale odour, the beige glow of the lamplight at night and the unbearable fustiness of the furniture. I couldn't stand it.

"Where have you been? Where's the car? Have you heard from Dad? Why hasn't he called? I'm worried he's dead, Alex! Is he dead? If he's dead, you have to tell me!"

"Give me a minute to dry off please, Mum," I said, trying to dart past her to get to the bathroom. A piece of chicken fell out from under my coat as I nudged by her, and she seized it at once, holding it up with a look of distaste plastered all over her face.

"What the hell is this, then? Oh my god, it's meat! Meat! What's happened to you, Alex?"

I lamented the loss of the chicken instantly, knowing that nothing short of a nuclear attack would make her relinquish her grip on it now.

"Nothing, nothing, I just really need to dry off," I said, marching down the hallway and into the wash-room. Mum followed close behind me, knocking on the door repeatedly as I turned the hot tap on so I could have a bath. It wasn't the mud I wanted to wash off - it was the intolerable odour of the house.

I could still hear the rain outside, and I opened the window as wide as it would go, gazing out at the back yard and drinking deeply of the cool night air. The clouds had blotted out the stars, but the moon was just visible through the grey haze of rain, and warm tears began to pool at the corners of my eyes at the sight of it. It was a strange sensation, as there was no noise coming out of my mouth whatsoever, no shaking of shoulders or wresting of garments. Just warm water, trembling on the rims of my eyes and running down my cheeks in long, slow-moving lines.

"Somewhere out there
Beneath the pale moonlight…"

The water gurgled out of the taps, drowning out the moans my mother was making outside the door, and I squeezed an entire container of Matey bubble bath into the churning white torrents of water, regardless of the impact it had on the environment. Then I undressed and sat on the edge of the bath, dipping the tips of my fingers into the soft, warm plateau of foam. It was the worst feeling in the world, being home after such an adventure, and if I hadn't been blind drunk at the time I might have sneaked into Mother's room, found my passport, packed a bag and never looked back.

"Alex, what on earth is going on? What are you singing in there? Is everything alright? Where did you get that chicken from? Where's Dad's coat?"

I wiped the foam onto my knee, and it rolled down slowly, settling on my leg-hair. There was another flash of lightning outside, and I was suddenly very proud of myself for traversing the storm so bravely. How desperately I wished to be back outside – even if I were in danger. I picked up a box of chicken, put it in the sink and sat beside it on the closed toilet lid, picking out the largest piece and tearing into it with insatiable lust. I felt like screaming, crying, bearing my soul to the world like Michael Jackson in Earth Song, and as I ate, I thought of all I had been through to find her, how easily she was lost. Could it really be true that I would never see her again?

Suddenly the thunder made a tremendous sound, as if one continent of the earth had been dropped upon another, and I walked to the window, letting the rain settle on my naked shoulders. She must be home by now, stacking the DVDs I gave her onto some decorative little shelf, or perhaps even taking a bath. Would it occur to her to look out of her bathroom window? To wonder if I were looking up at the night sky and thinking of her?

"Someone's thinking of me
And loving me tonight!"

The thought that she might love me excited me greatly, and I leaned out of the window, letting the tiny wet fingers of the rain caress my skin. Clutching the windowsill, I closed my eyes and imagined her standing at her own bathroom window, her silver-wet figure glowing in the moonlight. Then I took one hand from the windowsill and braced myself against the radiator. As if driven by some kind of sick sixth sense, my mother chose that moment to burst in through the door.

"Alexander Warren, what *are* you doing!"

The shame, the rage, the fury I felt as she rushed out again cannot be described. Is the human brain built to process such episodes of unbridled trauma? Traumas so great that they linger in the memory for years before even *beginning* to settle into the realm of the subconscious? I had two choices – to go out and face her, or stay where I was and act as if none of it had happened. The bath was about a quarter foam now, and the rest of the chicken I had been eating still lay in the sink. There was no enjoying the bath now, I decided, but I got in anyway. I had meant to spend a few moments in it then go explain myself to mother, but once immersed in the water's warm embrace, I found it very difficult to get back out, surveying the voluminous mounds of foam as though I were a miniature mountain explorer. Meanwhile, I could hear her shouting down the hallway.

"I was worried about him! I thought he'd slipped in the bath and drowned! Why was he doing that? Why didn't he answer?" This was beyond a disaster – it was the end of life as I knew it. I reached over to the sink for another piece of chicken, and as I did so, a huge swathe of bath suds spattered down the back of Dad's coat.

"What is he *doing* in there?" she screeched. It was then that I decided not to come out of the bath for at least a day. I had enough food to last me for a few days, and water from the tap to drink. I could empty the tub out and sleep in it tonight, covering myself up with a towel. The only problem was the lack of a lock on the door. Mum had always refused to put one on in case someone collapsed from the heat and knocked themselves unconscious on the sink, and until tonight we had operated on an honour system that nobody would try to open the door if someone else was in. That was down the drain now, along with any respect my mother might have previously had for me.

"Why are you shouting at *me*, woman?" George cried out down the corridor, and I felt an intense satisfaction that he was stuck with her while I was safe in the bathroom. I immersed my head under water, but above the rush of my blood and the thrum of the copper pipes, their voices could still be heard. I could no longer think of The Woman In The Red Coat, or anything else. I simply wanted to lay here, staring at the ceiling forever. I wondered how much longer I would have to stay under the water in order to die, and if it hadn't been for the sudden worry that water might get stuck in my ears, I might have found out. Remembering the time I had spent a whole night with earache after jumping into a swimming pool, I sat back up abruptly with a splash that set my mother screaming. I was no longer worried about the suds spilling all over Dad's coat. I dried myself, cleaned my teeth, brushed my hair and wrapped a towel around my waist. Then I grabbed the chicken. My mother's good opinion no longer concerned me, and when I heard the front door slam, I hoped it was the storm finally become avenger, here to sweep the dust and filth out of the house. It wasn't. It was my father.

I listened at the door as she started her sordid little story. Soon, there was a knock at the door, and I sat on the floor with my back to it, cradling the box of chicken in both arms. The batter still looked delicious, and I peeled a piece of it off, nibbling away at it miserably.

"Alex, where's the Mercedes?"

I didn't answer, shoving a whole chicken fillet in my mouth and bracing one foot against the side of the radiator to stop him getting in.

"Alex, what are you *doing* in there?!" Mother cried, as though she were grieving.

"Alex – where's the Mercedes?" Dad roared. "Where is it? Where's my CAR?"

I stuck out my other foot and dragged Dad's coat towards me, marvelling at how dry it was already. I draped it over my knee and took a closer look at it, noticing there was a little zipper along the collar. Intrigued, I pulled at the zip to find a pocket, and thrusting my hand in, discovered a small orange parcel wrapped in cellophane. I opened it up to find that it was a detachable hood.

I looked back on the day's events. Following the girl from the bus down a stormy road, getting soaked to the skin on the high street in search of an umbrella, and all the while, having the world's most expensive waterproof hood nestling millimetres away from the nape of my rain-drenched neck. Not only had I never noticed it – *Dad* hadn't either. For all his crowing about that jacket, he had never even noticed it had a hood. It was too much. I started to laugh out loud.

"What the hell are you laughing at, you maniac?"

The distress in Dad's voice was enough to make me laugh again. This man who knew everything, who only chose the best, who could tell you the time from looking at the position of the sun in the sky – this unemployed shyster who didn't even have the sense to use the world's most expensive coat in the way it was supposed to be used. What was the point of having the best if you didn't know how to use it? He was a fool, an idiot, one of life's big losers. But I had found it – after a single day, I had discovered the secret of the hood. Who was he then, to tell me what to do a moment longer? I laughed and laughed and laughed.

"Where's my Mercedes, you miserable little wretch? Did you sell it?" Dad shouted, trying the door handle. He shoved the door open and I yelled out "No!" pushing back against him with all my strength.

"Alex Warren, you open this door at once! Open this door or you'll regret it!" Dad cried. I screamed at him to stop, but it was no use. He was by far the stronger man, and if I'd been able to stand up and push back on the door with both my arms, I might have kept him out forever, but he had the advantage and there was no use denying the fact.

"No! No! I'm coming out, just let me get dressed," I shouted, realising a moment afterwards that everything but my boxer shorts and the waterproof jacket were soaked through. I put them on, took the remaining piece of chicken from the box in case someone should try to throw it away, and stepped out of the door.

"What in the name of god do you think you're doing?" my father yelled. "Are you some kind of pervert or what?" He pushed me against the wall and held me there while my mother screamed at him to stop. "What kind of funny business is this? Where's my car, you rotten little brat? Where is it?" I struggled to free myself from his grasp, twisting about until he only had hold of the coat. I ran into the kitchen in my underwear, still holding the chicken, and Mother pursued me, growling. It was horrifying – beyond anything imaginable.

The lightning outside flashed once, twice as I rummaged through the kitchen drawer to find some cling film to wrap up my chicken so that I could freeze it and save it for later before she confiscated it. Then Mum screamed, "He's got a knife!" and Dad ran in again with the jacket still in his hand, approaching me as if he were a matador heading toward a bull.

"What are you doing, Alex?" he asked, as if speaking to someone rather dangerous.

"I'm looking for some cling film," I said, plainly, my hand still in the drawer. "I want to freeze my chicken."

"What are you talking about? Where's my CAR, Alex?" Dad yelled, charging at me and covering my head with the jacket. I'd found the cling film at this stage, and had enough time to strike him with it a few times before he pulled me onto the floor, restricting my breathing most effectively.

"Get 'im Bill! Get 'im!" my mother shrieked. Even while fighting for my life I was *horrified* that she had taken his side, to say that Dad was the one who had attacked me, and called me all kinds of names for no good reason. It was he who had always stopped me from going where I liked, meeting girls, playing games with my friends and attending school. Him, my mum, and my brother George. I pulled the coat out of Dad's hands and draped it over myself as Mother screamed and screamed, the lightning illuminating her face. Dad snatched it back off me immediately.

"Give me that! Now, you listen to me. I want to know where my car is, and I want to know now."

"Go away!"

"I swear to god, if you've done anything to my car, I'll never forgive you for it. You'll never drive again – you'll be stuck here forever. You don't have any money. You don't have anything – no job, no woman, no car, and no life. You wouldn't last five minutes without us, you bloody drip!" he shouted.

"That's not true! I've got a girlfriend! She loves me and I love her! You can't tell me what to do anymore, Father. I'm leaving home, and this time I mean it!"

"Ha, ha, ha!" Dad laughed, clearly blind drunk, "That'll be the day! You'll never leave this house! Not even when you're dead! Never! NEVER!"

He spoke these words as though they were a curse.

"You owe me for that coat by the way," he said. "Don't think you're getting away with that one. Now go to your room, and don't come out until you're ready to tell me where my car is."

Utterly defeated, I did as he had ordered, trudging past my tutting mother, who for the first time in decades was clinging to my father's side, as if she were somehow titillated by the disgraceful dressing-down he'd just given her vulnerable, half-clothed son. George murmured something at me as I passed his bedroom, and I thought I sensed sympathy in his voice, but it disappeared soon afterward, and by the time I reached my bedroom, I was in floods of tears. Dad was right. If he took that £170 off me, I'd have nothing left – I'd spent every pound I had in a single day, and would be reliant on them for every penny from that day forward.

That was the last time I ever left the house. At first I couldn't answer Father's questions about the car because I was crying too hard. Later on, it was the way he kept on asking me, in a voice as utterly barren of kindness as the moon is of life. Finally, it was because he stopped asking. I imagine that the car was stolen from the lay-by where I'd left it, but for some reason Dad never did report it to the police. No doubt he'd broken some law or other regarding the upkeep. It really didn't concern me. Nothing did for a long time afterward.

Chapter Eight

How do you describe twenty years spent devoid of all substance, kindness and company, without driving your audience to suicide? Apart from the odd walk around the garden when it rained, I spent my life indoors after that night, dividing my time between watching the ever-growing numbers of romantic comedies churned out by Hollywood and learning how to make virtual reality videogames. By the time true virtual reality was affordable to the public, I was pushing fifty, but it was worth the wait to finally get Ms Ryan to one side and show her how a real man kissed! My first game was a VR re-vamp of 'Maid in Manhattan', with Daryl Hannah (from her 'Splash' era) playing J.Lo's role and Cary Grant replacing Ralph Fiennes. It was a modest success in niche circles, but even with the added thrill of an impossible intergenerational romance, something about it left me cold. You see, I never did forget the wonderful smile that The Woman In The Red Coat had given me that rainy night on the Ipswich train.

It's starting to get light out, and the birds outside are making a strange noise, crying "No, No, No, No, No!" Time to do the final room. The place I've spent my life. Emptied of all its miscellany, it looks innocent enough - a box with a sink in it, really, now that my bed's been broken up and disposed of.

The anterior room has a large window facing the front lawn.

I can't do this anymore. You see, the problem is those gravestones. What if I dragged Dad's old sledgehammer out of the conservatory and started smashing them to pieces? They're only stones after all, you can't get too sentimental over these things if you want to move forward

164

with your life.

An open fireplace forms the focal point of the room, with its ornate tiles, decorated in the art nouveau style.

I look around the room and see myself ageing as though I were walking through some twisted hall of mirrors. That slender young man, with his luminous skin and long, blonde hair has gone. There's something supernatural about youth that you can't quite put your finger on – it enchants everything – I mean, not just your face, but your ideas about how life should be. I spent the best years of mine holed up in this room, going over and over that perfect day until I found a way to make it real again.

In 'Summer's Lease' it's raining all the time. I spent years recreating the ambience of a summer thunderstorm right down to the last detail, and I've had a few global mentions from the games industry – it's a niche thing really, but every now and then some money comes in from my agent. Not much, but it's enough to tide me over until I sell the house. Dad and Mum were never interested in my success, of course. They wanted things to stay the way they'd always been, and so they did – for as long as they could, anyway. If there's such thing as heaven, I'm sure they've passed it up in order to linger on in these doorways, peering out of the windows at the grey stones in the garden. I'm the only one of them who can't stay on here for good. Who would bury me – a workman? It would be too much.

One of the things people remark upon when they enter the world of 'Summer's Lease' is how beautiful my version of Ipswich looks, not despite its faults, but *because* of them. It took me years of exposure to the picture-perfect worlds in films to begin to yearn for the flawed, cold reality of the city I'd left behind. Over the years, as I looked back over that day spent out in the rain, I came to see how the scruffy old couples had been holding hands despite their gruesome faces, remember the wonder in the eyes of the snot-nosed brats and the charming eccentricities of the local accents I'd found so repulsive. I missed it all desperately. And so, I made it happen again.

As comprehensive as the Virtual Ipswich in 'Summer's Lease' was, my crowning achievement was The Woman In The Red Coat herself. I'd stared at her face for so long that night on the train that its every line was etched in my memory by the time I'd recovered enough from my disagreement with Dad to think about her properly. I spent five years perfecting the Virtual Reality version of her. It took a whole month to calibrate the gap between her teeth until it was just wide enough to fit a pencil eraser into. Detail by detail, a millimetre at a time, I found the exact dimensions of her curls, scoured the internet for her cheap red coat, and simulated every combination of height and weight imaginable until she was standing right there in front of me on the train again. Her voice was the hardest thing to perfect, and it took me until I was forty-four to get every last detail in place. She was an instant hit in the VR games community, and it didn't take long for one of my fans to track down her real life counterpart.

Her name is Jennifer Martin, and I'm meeting her next week at Ipswich train station. I'm a shadow of the man I used to be in most respects – bald as a coot, diabetic, blind in one eye and two stone overweight. No doubt she's piled on the pounds herself, I'm under no illusions about that, but I want to know everything there is to know about her, and I think she will feel the same way about me. Our youth is long gone now. No doubt while we're walking along the platform hand in hand, some young upstart will point at us and laugh, but I'll be too busy rehearsing my proposal to notice. I'm convinced she'll say yes! It would be the perfect ending to our story.

Well, this house isn't going to sell itself, and I've got another rush of adrenaline coming on so strong it feels like I could do anything. In a minute I'm going to go and get that sledgehammer – drag it across the lawn, and smash those gravestones of theirs to smithereens. I'll push the rubble into the ditch, cut down some weeds and throw them over it all. The early hours are the perfect time for it, nobody driving past and a sense of new beginnings in the air. The oldest stones should be easy given their condition. Uncle Jack's was flimsy to begin with, and Grandad's has already fallen over. As for the rest of them – George, Mum, Dad, I'll wait until the rain stops before I do theirs. Maybe that way they'll finally notice that I'm crying.

Lightning Source UK Ltd.
Milton Keynes UK
UKOW04f1403300915

259569UK00002B/18/P